Candy can tell you a lot about a person. . . .

The door opens and there he is again, but this time I know his name: Marcus. He has to pass right by where I'm sitting to get to the teacher. *Ignore him.* My brain is trying to stay on task, but my hand seems to have a mind of its own. My next pass is so wiggly that it looks like a wave is breaking right in the middle of my canvas. I peek at the front of the room, where Marcus is handing an envelope to Miss Beans. I will him to look my way, but he doesn't. He waits while Miss Beans writes something on a piece of paper then folds it and gives it back to him. He turns, making me duck. *Calm down.* My next pass of the brush is even worse. The pileup of gesso is starting to look more mountain range-ish and less wave-ish. I keep my head down as Marcus walks toward me. He slows as he gets close. His hand hovers over the corner of my desk and then he's past and out the door before I can register what's happened. The grape Jolly Rancher sitting on my desk is the only evidence that he was here. I fold my hand over the candy and pull it into my lap before anyone can see.

OTHER BOOKS YOU MAY ENJOY

Heather Hepler

the cupcake Queen

speak

An Imprint of Penguin Group (USA) Inc.

SPEAK

Published by the Penguin Group

Penguin Group (USA) Inc., 345 Hudson Street, New York, New York 10014, U.S.A.

Penguin Group (Canada), 90 Eglinton Avenue East, Suite 700, Toronto, Ontario, Canada M4P 2Y3
(a division of Pearson Penguin Canada Inc.)

Penguin Books Ltd, 80 Strand, London WC2R 0RL, England

Penguin Ireland, 25 St Stephen's Green, Dublin 2, Ireland (a division of Penguin Books Ltd)

Penguin Group (Australia), 250 Camberwell Road, Camberwell, Victoria 3124, Australia
(a division of Pearson Australia Group Pty Ltd)

Penguin Books India Pvt Ltd, 11 Community Centre, Panchsheel Park, New Delhi - 110 017, India

Penguin Group (NZ), 67 Apollo Drive, Rosedale, North Shore 0632, New Zealand
(a division of Pearson New Zealand Ltd)

Penguin Books (South Africa) (Pty) Ltd, 24 Sturdee Avenue, Rosebank, Johannesburg 2196, South Africa

Registered Offices: Penguin Books Ltd, 80 Strand, London WC2R 0RL, England

First published in the United States of America by Dutton Children's Books,
a division of Penguin Young Readers Group, 2009
Published by Speak, an imprint of Penguin Group (USA) Inc., 2010

7 9 10 8

CIP DATA IS AVAILABLE.

ISBN 978-0-525-42157-3 (hc)

Speak ISBN 978-0-14-241668-6

Designed by Irene Vandervoort
Printed in the United States of America

For Harrison, with love

the
cupcake
Queen

chapter one

The fact that I wasn't surprised when my mother handed me the sheet pan filled with pink frosted cupcakes is possibly more disturbing than the cupcakes themselves. They're pink, I mean *pink*. Pink cupcake papers, pink cupcakes, pink frosting, pink sprinkles, and now pink rosebuds. It's like someone drank a whole bottle of Pepto-Bismol and then threw up in six dozen clumps. I can't even laugh about it with anyone, because anyone who would think this is as funny as I do is three hundred miles away. And maybe three hundred miles doesn't seem like much, but when you still have two and a half years before you can drive—and that's only if my mother let's me have time off from decorating cupcakes to get my license—three hundred miles might as well be three million. All I know is I get to spend the next hour putting exactly fourteen miniature pink sugar rosebuds on each of six dozen cupcakes (that's 1,008 rosebuds in case you're counting, and I am) while everyone I know who might think this is as crazy as I do is three billion miles away doing exactly what I wish I were doing right now. *Anything other than this.*

"How's it going?" Gram asks, pushing through the swinging door into the kitchen. I shrug, something I've gotten really good at. She pulls open one of the big refrigerator doors and sticks most of her upper body inside. I can hear her talking, but the oven fans and whir of the mixer muffle her words.

"What did you say?" I ask when she closes the refrigerator.

"I said your beach cupcakes are a big hit."

I nod and keep placing the tiny rosebuds on the cupcakes, slowly spinning the turntable as I go to make sure they're even. I know my mother will check. Gram puts a tray of vanilla cupcakes on the counter beside me. She lifts one. "These are my favorite," she says, holding up a blue-frosted cupcake with a tiny sailboat on top. "Of course the kids like the crabs— they have more icing." She hums as she takes the tray of cupcakes through the door to the front of the bakery. I sigh and use my tweezers to pick up another rosebud and place it on a cupcake.

Cupcake.

Six months ago, if someone had said the word *cupcake*, it probably wouldn't have even registered. I mean, sure, who doesn't like them? But a whole bakery devoted just to cupcakes? I asked my mother that when she told me. "Nothing else?" She just laughed, like it was the funniest thing I'd said all day. I didn't quite believe it until I saw the man putting the final touches on the lettering on the window: THE CUPCAKE QUEEN.

"Penny." I jump at the sound of my name and accidentally jab the cupcake with the tweezers, leaving a hole. My mother sighs behind me. "You're off in dreamland again," she says. Not true. More like nightmareland. She whisks the mutilated cupcake off the turntable and drops it into the trash, replacing it with a fresh one. "Here," she says, holding out her hand for the tweezers. I watch as she expertly places fourteen tiny rosebuds all over the top of the cupcake before trading it for another. "You just need to focus," she says, completing three more in the time it would have taken me to do one. She hands the tweezers back to me. *Focus.* My mother is quite possibly the most focused person I know. I feel her focusing on my hands as I struggle to pick up another rosebud with my tweezers. It slips and I end up breaking it. The buzz of her cell phone saves me from another lecture on the importance of attention to details.

She listens for a while after saying hello. "Oh no, it's okay. We'll manage," she says finally, looking at the clock above my head. "Just feel better." She taps her free fingers against the counter. "Just let me know." She flips her phone shut with a click. "Great," she says, her voice flat.

Gram pushes back through the door with another empty tray. "Lizzie, those summer cupcakes are going like hotcakes." Ever since we moved from Manhattan, population 1.6 million, to Hog's Hollow, population 5,134, my mother has been Lizzie. In New York, people called her Elizabeth or Ms. Lane.

"That was Jeannie," my mother says, holding up her cell phone. "She's sick." My mother sighs again. Probably her tenth sigh in the last hour. "There is no way I can do the setup by myself. I mean, there are the flowers and the china and the linens . . ."

"Don't forget the cupcakes," Gram says. I have to duck my head so that my mother doesn't see me smile.

"Yes, Mother," she says, "the cupcakes."

That's one thing I do like about Hog's Hollow: my grandmother. She's the only person I know who isn't afraid of my mother. Even my father's afraid of my mom.

"I just can't do it all alone. Jeannie goes back to college in less than a week." She stares at the phone, as if willing Jeannie to call again to say that she's fine, she'll be right in.

"Take Penny," Gram says, pulling another sheet pan of cupcakes from the refrigerator.

"What?" we both say. My mother looks over at me in time to see me break another sugar rosebud.

"I don't think she—" my mother begins.

"I don't think I—" I say.

"You'll be fine," Gram says, pushing the door to the front open with her hip. She flashes me a grin before it swings shut, trapping me in the kitchen with my mother.

"You'll be fine," my mother tells me. I can't tell whether she's saying this to herself or me. After loading the van with cupcakes, extra sugar rosebuds, four huge bouquets of flowers in various shades of (yep, you guessed it) pink, a stack of white tablecloths, and several totes of rented plates and silverware and glasses, my mother got to work on me. First I had to endure *the scrutiny*. I should be used to it by now, but I never am. Let me paint the scene. Me: black jeans, black Chucks, black T-shirt. Mousy-brown hair pulled into a low ponytail. Burt's Bees on my lips. Blue mascara on my eyelashes. *I know*, but I read in *Cosmo* that it's supposed to make your eyes look more dramatic, and I can use all the help I can get. The problem is not so much me, but my mother. She's a firm believer in looking pulled together at all times, and it seems I'm the opposite of that. Maybe I'm pulled apart. So, there I am, a vision in black with flour streaks on my jeans (and probably my face) and my mother is tilting her head at me, trying to see if I make the cut to go to the country club. And I see her thinking no, but then realizing that she has no choice. It's either take me with her where she can keep an eye on me, or take Gram and leave me to run the bakery *alone*. And, then there's another sigh. "Let's see what I can do," she says, walking to the back office, where she keeps her purse.

Fast-forward ten minutes and I'm sitting in the passenger seat of the van with what she could do all over me. New ponytail.

Higher up, like a cheerleader's. Clean T-shirt—white, not black. A scrub at my eyes dislodged the blue mascara and a swipe of lipstick at my mouth makes it look like I've been sucking on a cherry Popsicle all afternoon.

"Don't rub at your lips," my mother says, and I lower my hand into my lap. "This is a great opportunity for you." She steers across the road and into the parking lot of the Hog's Hollow Country Club. "There'll be a lot of girls there your age."

I stare at the side of her face, and she looks over at me. Seeing my expression, she laughs. "Penny," she says, turning into a parking space at the side of the building marked DELIVERIES. "Don't tell me you didn't know." She looks at me again and can tell I didn't know. "Fourteen rosebuds, fourteen years."

She's talking to me like I'm five, but it's only because I don't want to believe what she's saying. I thought I had a good two weeks before I was going to have to meet anyone. I mean, I've met people. A lot of Gram's friends who stop by on their morning walks to get a breakfast cupcake (one of my inventions) and some gossip. And a lot of my mother's old friends from when she grew up here. But I've been able to duck anyone my age, sliding into the bakery through the back and staying in the kitchen all day before heading home to stay in my room all night. I keep telling myself if I pretend I don't live here, I don't. I spend most nights IM'ing my friends back in the City. They're keeping me up-to-date with everything so when I move back I won't have missed too much.

"Earth to Penny," my mother says, actually waving her fingers in front of my face. "Look," she says. "Don't be nervous."

"Who's nervous?" I ask. And the truth is, it's only partly nerves. Mostly it's that I don't want this. Any of it. I don't want to start a new school and make new friends. I don't want to have a mother who runs a bakery called The Cupcake Queen instead of the cool art gallery in Chelsea. I don't want to live in Hog's Hollow instead of in the Village. And I definitely do not want to carry six dozen pink cupcakes covered in pink rosebuds into the ballroom of the Hog's Hollow Country Club so that some fourteen-year-old girl named Charity can have a HAPPY SWEET FOURTEEN, as the banner over the entrance says.

"Come on, Penny," my mother says. "Try to make the best of it." She winks when she says it, and I can kind of see the mother that I used to know. The one who would walk with me through Central Park even when it was three below zero. The one who would take me all the way uptown to Zabar's so we could get a cup of the best hot chocolate in the whole world. Then she blows it. "Just try to focus, okay?"

"Yeah," I say. "Focus." As I slide the first box of cupcakes out of the rack in the back of the van and start to carry it inside, I want to tell her that focusing isn't the problem. It's what I'm focusing on that sucks.

chapter two

I have never done this be-
fore, but the job sounds simple enough. Go in, set tables with
tablecloths, silverware, napkins, forks, etc. Set up cake stands,
add cupcakes, check rosebuds, leave. Usually Mom does this
alone, or if she needs help, she'll call Jeannie. Jeannie, who is in
college. Jeannie, who has naturally blond hair, a red MINI
Cooper, and a boyfriend named Stuart. But instead of Jeannie,
my mom has me. And Mom tells me "It'll be fine" so many
times that when I pull the last box of cupcakes out of the van,
my hands are shaking badly enough to knock off some of the
rosebuds. By the time I get inside it sounds like I have a cardboard box full of marbles instead of cupcakes.

"Just put it over there, Penelope," my mother says over her
shoulder. I know now that something is up, because my mother
never calls me Penelope. It's unfortunate, too, considering
my name. My father, Peter Lane, is a huge Beatles fan. In ad-

dition to a cat named Rita (as in lovely Rita meter maid), a dog named Lucy (in the sky with diamonds), and a tank full of fish named after the band members themselves, he decided that he should pay tribute to the Fab Four with his daughter's name, too. Yep, I'm Penny Lane. I'm told it could be worse, but no one who says that can actually tell me how.

I place the box full of cupcakes on the table and stand there, waiting for my mother to finish talking to a very large woman with very big hair. Manhattan is filled with women with simple, stylish hair. From what I've seen of Hog's Hollow, the trend here seems to be the more, the better. More hair, more makeup, more jewelry. I start pulling the napkins out of their wrappers. I know a trick to make them spiral into a star pattern instead of just sitting there in a stack. You take a glass and lay it on its side on top of the stack and then twist. I used to do it all the time for openings at Mom's gallery. Chelsea art openings serve sushi and little crackers covered with slivers of cucumber and spoonfuls of caviar. Here in Hog's Hollow it's pink cupcakes and punch made from ginger ale and fruit juice, and watermelons hollowed out to look like baskets to hold little balls of watermelon. There's something disturbing about gutting a piece of fruit and then reshaping and replacing the guts like it's art.

"Penelope, there's someone I want you to meet." Again with the Penelope. I walk over to where she is standing with the big-hair woman and a girl wearing enough pink to make

Barbie look somber. "This is Mrs. Wharton, and this"— dramatic pause—"is her daughter, Charity." I take Mrs. Wharton's hand, which feels like limp lettuce, and smile at her daughter.

"Um, it's Penny," I say softly. Charity looks at me briefly and then past me. I can't stop staring at her hair. It's the same color as mine, but where mine tends toward wavy on good days and frizzy on bad days, Charity's is shiny and smooth and seems to almost glow. The way she keeps shaking her head slightly to make it move makes me understand that she knows exactly how great her hair is.

"It's my Charity's special day," Mrs. Wharton says, and at first it doesn't register what she is talking about. Finally, re- membering the sign out front, I mumble, "Happy birthday." Charity makes her hair ripple again and offers me a cold smile that nearly matches the ice carving on the buffet table. Who has an ice carving of herself?

"Charity is going into the ninth grade, too," my mother says to me. When I don't respond, she continues. "Penelope?" She looks over at me. "Penny is just a little bit nervous."

And for the first time in a while, my mother is right. I am nervous. Back home, I had friends. Not a lot, but enough, and then a whole group of sorta-friends. Here, well, other than my mom (who I don't count) and Gram (who I do, but who's a lit- tle old to be attending high school) and my cat, Oscar (there's no Beatles reference—I put my foot down), I have no one.

"Oh, don't you worry, dearie," Mrs. Wharton says. "Charity will show you around."

Charity smiles again, but as soon as our mothers turn their attention away from us, her smile fades. She looks at me as if the effort of just being near me is painful. "So, you're new," Charity says, but the way she says it is almost like she just said, "So, you smell like sweaty socks." I just nod, wishing I could sound as cool and funny on the outside as I think I do on the inside. "Well," Charity says, looking at me, waiting for me to say *something*. "Nice talking to you, Patty." I start to correct her, but she just walks away, giving me this half wave with the back of her hand.

I decide that instead of just standing beside my mother, wishing I was anywhere but there, I'll start setting up. My mother is so into something Mrs. Wharton is saying about the chamber of commerce that she doesn't notice what I'm doing. I start with the cake stands. I try to make as little noise as possible as I fish through the box holding the various pieces. There are six plastic disks, two of each size, and then four columns that support each disk, forming two tiny towers each perfect for three tiers of cakes or, in this case, three dozen cupcakes. If you're having a hard time picturing it, think the Parthenon, but smaller and made out of plastic. I start fitting the two towers together, setting them up on either end of the dessert table. I fill the bottom two tiers first, thinking that I don't want them to topple over from being too top-heavy. I have filled both towers by the time my mother finishes talking and Mrs. Wharton is clapping her hands for everyone's attention.

"Thanks, Penny," my mother says, stepping around the table to where I am quickly replacing rosebuds on some of the cupcakes. To my mother's credit, her smile only slips the tiniest bit when she sees what I'm doing. "Penny, go ahead and set the rest of the cupcakes out on the platters around the cake stands."

Just as I am carefully transferring the last of the cupcakes to the trays, Mr. Wharton starts walking toward us. As big as Mrs. Wharton is, Mr. Wharton is bigger. And I don't mean just a little bigger. I mean like he left the town of Three Hundred Pounds and is careening toward the city of Four Hundred Pounds. His wife looks at her watch. "Let's all gather around the birthday girl for a photo. That'll give us time to get some food before we start the fashion show."

I back up from the table so that I can see the stage they have set up at the front of the room. This gives my mother enough room to step up to the table to adjust the cupcakes that I had set out. Mr. Wharton walks over and pokes one of his fingers into a cupcake, stealing a glob of frosting. My mother smiles stiffly at him. He winks at her and turns to watch as Charity has her picture taken from every possible angle.

"Okay, Charity, you go first," her mother says. But Charity is already halfway across the floor and coming toward the table. Something tells me Charity *always* goes first.

"Hi, sweetheart," Mr. Wharton says when Charity walks up to dish up some fruit and select a cupcake. She barely glances in his direction. Mr. Wharton is not about to be separated from the food, so instead of going to stand beside his wife, he decides to lean against the dessert table. Maybe if an average-size person had leaned against it then everything would have been fine, but as I already said, Mr. Wharton is not average-size.

The rest all happens as if in slow motion. As the table tilts under Mr. Wharton's weight, the upper tiers of the cupcake stands begin to teeter. My mother makes a grab for the tower on one end, attempting to keep it upright by pushing on one of the columns. The upper two tiers tip sideways and then topple. My mother catches half a dozen cupcakes with her hands and a couple more with her face. The second tower is positioned right in front of Charity, who at that very moment has her hand poised over a particularly large cupcake. Charity apparently doesn't have the hand-eye coordination of my mother. She ends up wearing a dozen or more cupcakes like a hat while half a dozen more slide slowly down the front of her dress.

"Oh my goodness," is all Mrs. Wharton can manage. She hustles over to the table, pushing her husband, who has also been hit by a few flying cupcakes. Unfortunately, instead of pushing him out of the way, she pushes him into the table. Now, I know those kinds of tables have to be built to hold a lot of weight, but I don't think the builders had someone like Mr.

Wharton in mind. When his right hip hits the end of the table, it buckles slightly—enough to tip over one of the melon baskets and send the punch bowl sliding down the tablecloth.

"Oh my goodness," Mrs. Wharton repeats. She grabs at the punch bowl as it slides toward her. The bowl bumps against her stomach, which stops it, but the contents of the bowl keep going, splashing up and over her, turning the whole front of her white dress pink. All of the extra cupcakes begin sliding along the length of the table, too. Trying to prevent more damage, Mr. Wharton grabs the closest end of the table—the lower end—and lifts it up. Unfortunately, he lifts too fast and too far, sending *everything* flying. Mr. Wharton snatches a couple of the cupcakes that shoot in his direction and stuffs one into his mouth. The forks that my mother had so carefully arranged in a circle become dangerous projectiles. The glasses—luckily not glass at all, but heavy plastic—clatter loudly to the floor.

"Save the melon!" Mrs. Wharton shouts over the noise, as if saving one piece of fruit will make any difference. My mother manages to grab one of the melon boats, catching it like a football. The other upends right in front of Charity, sending balls of watermelon flying in every direction. I manage to snag a couple of the plates, but the rest of them crash to the ground. Some of them shatter, but others land on end and make lazy circles on the floor before flopping over. Not everyone ends up wearing some sort of food. Several girls manage to stay clean. I am one of them; something my mother is not likely to forget.

After a lot of apologies and promises to refund their money, my mother and I spend an embarrassing twenty minutes cleaning up the mess. About halfway through, Charity comes out of the bathroom, where she had fled immediately after the accident. She has a tablecloth clutched around her; her dress either abandoned in the trash or left for her mother to retrieve. Her mascara has left long trails of black on her cheeks, and her hair is matted. Her friends stay close to her as they walk past me. I bend to scoop up another handful of melon balls before I realize that the group of girls hasn't walked past after all but has stopped in front of me. Charity stands there, her pink high heels peeking out from under the tablecloth. I look at her and watch as a glob of pink frosting slowly slides from her hair and comes to rest on her shoulder. "I'll see you in school, Penny." She stares at me for several seconds without blinking. I start to stammer an apology, but she just shakes her head at me. She walks out, followed by her entourage, each of them pausing long enough to give me the ice stare.

"Great," I say, dropping the handful of melon balls into the empty box. "Now she remembers my name."

chapter three

Saying the ride back is a little uncomfortable would be like saying that walking across pieces of glass and then a pile of salt smarts a little. My mother is taking the sighing thing to a new level. It's at the point where I'm afraid she's going to hyperventilate. I tell her it's going to be okay. She just nods and keeps watching the road.

We ride in silence for the rest of the way into town. I stare out the window, seeing the big wooden sign for Hog's Hollow. WELCOME HOME, it says at the bottom. The brochures my mother keeps in the bakery describe about the rustic charm of the area. If *rustic* means "old," they're right. Main Street still has a whole section of cobblestone, and most of the store signs are made out of wood that's been carved and painted. When we lived in the City, my family used to go to the shore in the summer, to towns that are faux rustic. You can tell that they're not the real deal because everything seems a little too perfect. All the signs match; there are identical iron lampposts on every corner. Flowers are planted in barrels; trash cans have wooden boxes built around them. Even the McDonald's look rustic. They're like Hollywood studio sets. But Hog's Hollow isn't fake rustic, it's the real deal.

My mother turns down one of the side streets and swings around to the back of the bakery, where she parks near the Dumpster. I climb out and go to the back of the van and start sliding out boxes and crates and stacking them on the back porch. It takes only a few minutes to get everything inside. I start to put the cake stands in the dishwasher. "Just leave them," my mother says softly. "It's late."

We walk back out to the van and head to Gram's house, a Cape near the beach. I heard my mother talking to her on the phone before we left the City. "Just until we get settled," Mom said when Gram offered to let us live with her. Of course I'm not about to settle. Settling means staying. We turn onto the gravel road that takes us toward the water and the house. At the corner is a sign for JOY'S PHOTOGRAPHY STUDIO. Sometimes I hear Gram working down in the darkroom until late at night, and yet she's still up at dawn to get to the bakery. Even though she just turned sixty-five, she has more energy than my mother and me put together.

My mother pulls the van around the house and parks it in front of the garage. She looks at me for a long moment, but then she's out and walking toward the back porch before I can say anything. I hear the screen door snap shut behind her as she goes inside. I take my blue hoodie out of my backpack and pull it on before sliding out of the van and heading toward the path down to the water.

We got here in June, right after school was out. It was only going to be for the summer at first. Mom told me she just needed to get away, and I know that meant she needed to get away from my dad. And I hope that's all it is. Like they just need a break from each other.

For a long time I would hear them arguing when I was supposed to be sleeping. They'd fight about everything—my school, who left crumbs in the butter, whose turn it was to take Oscar to the vet. That was bad. But it was worse when they stopped. It was like as long as they were arguing, they cared. Once they stopped it seemed like everything stopped.

I'd like to say I saw it coming—the move, I mean. But the truth is, until she started hauling the suitcases out of the closet, I had no idea Mom had even been thinking about leaving the City. The only thing I noticed was that she notched up the intensity level a little. But with my mother, that's like increasing things from an 8 to a 10, so it's just more of more. I guess the other thing was that she went kind of crazy. But it was a quiet crazy, one that only I could see. She started obsessing about everything. Even simple decisions, like what kind of jam to buy at the store, seemed to have huge consequences in her mind. She would stand there, staring at the jars until I'd finally just pick one for her. It was right after that that I found the packet from the Hog's Hollow Chamber of Commerce on my mother's desk. Only a week later a moving van was double-parked in front of our apartment building and guys with names like STAN and PAUL stitched in red on their jumpsuits were hauling boxes of books and clothes down the stairs and out into the rain.

My dad moved out first. He told me the separation was good, because they needed time to heal. The problem was that they didn't tell me from what. He said everything was going to be fine, but he didn't bother to show up at the diner for our last breakfast. He just left a message on my mom's cell that something had come up and he was really sorry, but to call when we got there so he'd know we were safe. And I know something probably did come up and that the something was probably important, but sometimes I just wish the something important could be me.

And for the entire drive to Hog's Hollow, as I sat there in my mom's blue Toyota hatchback, I kept thinking about what my dad had said. That everything was going to be fine. And I realized maybe that's all we can hope for from life: fine. Not happy, not good, but just fine. And in my case "fine" is an acronym for Freakin' Irrational Nightmare Existence.

I take off my socks and shoes at the top of the stairs, roll my socks into balls, and shove them into the tops of my sneakers. The sand feels cool on my feet as I walk down toward the water. I stand at the edge of where the wet sand meets the dry and try

to figure out if the tide is going in or out. The wind is cold off
the water. It feels good after a whole day stuck inside, but it
raises goose bumps on my arms and makes me shiver.

About a month after we arrived, my mom did the whole we
need to have a talk thing. She brought me down to the beach
and I thought, *Finally, she's going to tell me what's going on,* but
instead she just talked about finding herself and her roots and
figuring out what was really important. When she said, "I'm
going to open a bakery," dumb me, I thought she meant in
New York. And while it was surprising, I wasn't really surprised. My mom has always been what she calls "vaguely artistic." I started to get excited as she talked about the bakery idea.
I pictured a tiny shop in SoHo that made specialty cakes and
got featured in the Food Section of the *New York Times*. Then
she told me the bakery wasn't going to be in the City at all, but
out here. Here, in Hog's Hollow, where they actually crown a
Hog Queen every fall.

If my life were a movie, I would have calmly outlined all the
reasons why a bakery would be a bad business move. I would
have told her why city life suits us better than life out here
in the sticks. But my life isn't a movie. Not even close. And I
wasn't calm and cool and convincing. Instead, I ran away. I
took off down the beach and ran until I couldn't run any more
and then I just collapsed on the sand and cried. The next thing
I did was e-mail my dad and beg him to talk some sense into
her. I wanted him to drive here and ask her to come back,

maybe even beg her to come back. Because opening a bakery seems really final, like the first step in their splitting up for good. But as much as I tried to fight it, on that day a summer turned into forever. That is, until I can figure out a way to convince my mother that we need to move back to the City.

I watch the water, still trying to figure out which way the tide is going. Every time I think I figure it out, it seems to change. I hear a dog running behind me. I turn to see him coming straight toward me, fast, kicking up sand as he goes, and all at once he is on me, big wet paws, big wet tongue. His paws are on my chest as he tries to lick my face. He's so happy that I just start laughing. It's the first time I've laughed in forever, and it feels strange in my mouth, like the first time I had sushi. Good, but weird. The dog backs off a bit and begins running around me in circles, making a chuffing sound in his throat. I bend and put out my hand, and he comes right to me again. I pet him, scratching behind his ears. His fur is thick and golden and damp from the ocean.

"Good boy," I say. He smells good, like seawater and salt, but also bad, like wet dog.

"Sam, no." I look up to see a guy running toward me and I stand up again. The dog, who I now know is Sam, sits down beside me and thumps his tail. "I'm so sorry," the guy says, reaching for Sam's collar. Sam leans into my legs, making me laugh. "Sam, no."

"It's okay," I say.

The guy looks at me. "He gets a little excited," he says. He smiles and pushes his curly brown hair back from his forehead. Even in the dim light, I can see that his eyes are really deep brown, like Sam's, and when he smiles, the corners crinkle.

"A little." I smile and bend down to pat Sam on the head. Sam keeps thumping his tail on the sand, making a weird sand angel with each swish.

"He likes you."

"I suspect that Sam likes everyone." I look up. The guy is watching me, and suddenly I'm self-conscious in my rolled-up jeans and my sandy hoodie. He smiles again and pushes up the sleeve of his sweatshirt. He has a braided leather bracelet on his wrist that slides down toward his hand when he moves his arm.

"Sam's actually pretty selective." Sam keeps pushing his head into my hand, petting himself on my fingers.

"Is he?" I bend and scratch Sam behind the ears again.

"He's a very good judge of character." He blushes slightly after he says it and pushes his hair off his forehead again. Sam thumps his tail once more and tears off down the beach. We hear him bark, but it's too dark to see him. "I guess I better—"

"I guess so," I say. He smiles again. *Crinkle.* He backs away and lifts a hand in my direction before turning and running after Sam.

"Bye," I say, but it's just to myself, because he's too far away to hear. I walk back to the steps and stuff my socks into my pockets before I slip on my high-tops, pushing the laces down inside of them. The kitchen light is on, but the rest of the house is dark. I walk quietly up onto the porch and settle into the glider. I lean my head back and close my eyes. I hear barking from way down the beach and smile, wishing I knew the guy's name and not just his dog's.

"It was awful." I can hear my mother in the kitchen. I hold still and listen.

"Tea?" Gram asks. I imagine her holding up the kettle as she asks. *Tea fixes everything,* she always says.

"Please," my mother says. Her voice sounds tired, more than ever. Ever since she came here, she sounds different, like just holding her body together and moving around is hard.

"Tell me everything," Gram says, and I cringe. It's enough that my mother thinks I'm a screwup. Not Gram, too. My mother does tell her everything. She doesn't even leave out Charity's parting comment, which I didn't think she had heard. And when she finishes, they're quiet. I hold my breath and wait, wondering what Gram will say. Wanting to know and not wanting to at the same time. And then I hear Gram laughing. She starts out soft and gets louder and louder until I can hear her gasping, and I know tears are rolling down her cheeks. It feels awful, hearing her laugh at me.

"Mother," Mom says, but Gram doesn't stop. And then I

hear a surprising thing. My mother starts laughing, too. Which just makes Gram laugh harder. "You should have seen her face." I wonder who they mean. Me?

"Oh, what I would have given to see that," Gram says. The laughing begins to die down, and I hear a lot of whoo's and sighs. This time happy ones.

"The look on Eugenia's face when the first cupcake hit her." My mother starts laughing again. I try to figure out who Eugenia is.

"And her daughter. What's her name?"

"Charity," my mother says, and I realize they are talking about Mrs. Wharton.

"Charity, oh yes. What a preposterous name for such a selfish family."

"Maybe Stingy was already taken."

"I was surprised when you got the call to do the cupcakes for her daughter's birthday," Gram says. "After everything . . ."

"I can't afford to be choosy. It's such a small town."

"I know, but still . . ." They are both quiet for a moment. "How was Penny with all of it?" Gram asks. I sit forward a little to listen, but all I hear is my mother's sigh, then silence.

"I don't know," my mother says finally. "I wish we didn't—" But then she stops talking, leaving me wondering what she wishes we didn't do. Move here? Open a bakery? Make a thousand pink cupcakes for Miss Ice Princess?

I lean back in the bench and swing my feet. I feel the rough wood pull at my hair. Even though I'm glad my mom's not mad at me, their laughter makes my stomach hurt. It may be selfish to think it, but I don't want my mom to be happy. The happier she is, the farther away my old life gets.

chapter four

The first day of school always gets me out of bed early. The first day of school at a *brand-new* school got me out of bed at 4 A.M. By the time I left Gram's house my room looked like a bomb had gone off in it. Every piece of clothing I owned was on either the floor or the bed. I checked my e-mail five times and tried unsuccessfully to find something to eat that wouldn't make me feel like yakking four times. I kept speeding up and then slowing down during the walk to school. I didn't want to be late, but I *really* didn't want to be too early, standing around and staring at my shoes while everyone else talks to one another and pretends not to see the new girl staring at her shoes. I managed to make it to the school office without actually making eye contact with anyone. It's like if I don't see them, they can't see me.

So, here's my theory. Every high school in the whole country has the same secretary working in the front office. She's usually about my mom's age or maybe a little older, like forty-ish. She's a little overweight, but she's trying to lose it and you know that because she always has a Diet Coke or a Slim-Fast shake on her desk, and her candy jar is filled with sugarless Jolly Ranchers. Her name is something no one names their kids anymore, like Esther or Geraldine or Margery. She wears clothes that are about ten years out-of-date, and around every holiday she brings out the theme sweatshirts, like the reindeer one with the light-up Christmas lights on his antlers. She has a calendar with sayings like HANG IN THERE with a picture of a kitten hanging from a branch. I might be wrong about all of this—I haven't been in that many schools—but I think I might be onto something here, because when I walk into the front office at Hog's Hollow High School, a woman with apple earrings and a cardigan with apples all over it is sipping a Diet Pepsi. I notice the sign on her desk reads CONSTANCE PITTMAN.

"Sign in," she says, tapping the clipboard on the counter. She takes it from me after I write down my name. "Penny Lane," she says, and I wait for it, the humming, the comments, but she just rolls her chair to one side and opens a file drawer. "Lane, Lane, Lane . . . Oh, here we are." She takes a folder from the drawer and drops it onto her desk. She slips a pink sheet out of the folder and glances at it. "Looks like you're with Madame Framboise for first period." She hands me the sheet and starts rummaging in another file. I scan the grid on the sheet and find first period. French I.

"I think maybe there's a mistake." I have to lean over the counter to make sure she can hear me. "I don't take French. I mean, I haven't. I take Spanish."

A bell rings. *Great. I'm late.* She flips through the pages and then starts at the beginning and goes through them more slowly. "Not here. Here we have French. I can't seem to find . . ." She sees a piece of blue paper in my folder and slides it free. "Well, I must have given you a locker already." She folds the sheet in half and hands it to me. "Memorize that and then destroy it." She seems so serious that I smile.

"Do I have to swallow it?"

She tilts her head and squints at me. "Why would you do that?"

"Never mind," I say. I fold the blue piece of paper, push it into the back pocket of my jeans, and follow the directions she gave me to find my first class. I stop at Room 110 and double-check my schedule. *French. Well, this should be interesting.* I turn the knob slowly and push open the door. As expected, every eye in the class is immediately on me and no longer on who I guess to be Madame Framboise.

"*Bonjour,*" she says. Okay, I know that one.

"*Bonjour,*" I mumble.

"Class," she says, turning back to them. There is a murmur through the room. Whispers of "She's new" filter toward me. I keep telling myself that it's no big deal, that I'll be moving back to New York soon and then this nightmare will be over.

"Class," Madame Framboise says again. Then she says something that sounds like *a cootie bean*, but that must mean "listen," because everyone gets quiet. She puts her hand out toward me and I start to put out my own, thinking she wants to shake it. *"Votre schedule,"* she says. I catch the last word and hand her my pink sheet. "Ah, Penny," she says, putting a stress on the end of my name so it sounds like she's saying "Pen Knee." There are more whispers and this time I hear "Pen Knee" thrown in. One girl toward the front says it in a particularly nasty way, and I recognize her from the birthday party. *Great.* "Pen Knee. *Prenez le_____.*" This one I have no idea. She repeats it. I can feel myself turning seventy-five shades of red.

"I don't—"

"En français," she says.

"I don't understand—"

"Vous ne comprenez pas."

Okay, I can do this. Comprenez. *Comprehend.* I shake my head.

She sighs, and the whispers start up again. "Take your seat."

The only free desk is one toward the back of the third row. I have to walk past Charity's friend, who slides her backpack into the aisle, making me step over it. Luckily, I'm ready for it. Unfortunately I'm not ready for friend number two about halfway back, who decides at that moment to stretch her leg. I only fall partway, catching myself on the edge of a desk.

"*Bon voyage?*" she asks, smiling.

I feel my face get hot and then the backs of my eyes get hot. *Do not cry,* I tell myself. I slide into the empty chair and pretend to study my schedule while everyone begins whispering again about someone named *Pen Knee.*

Somehow I make it through French. Then math, where it's a lot of stuff I already did in eighth grade. There don't seem to be any of Charity's friends in that class, but art class is another story. The whole back table is full of them. And there she is, Charity, right in the middle. I hear "Pen Knee" under their breath as I walk in. I find a seat near the window, next to a girl with dark hair with the tips dyed blue. She's wearing glasses with rhinestones in the corners. The teacher, Miss Beans, begins talking about all of the projects we are going to do this year. She seems nervous as she talks, and I wonder if she's new, too. One of the girls at the back table makes a coughing noise and in the middle says, "Pen." Another coughs, "Knee." And another, "Loser." Miss Beans looks at them for a long moment until they are quiet. How is it possible that after only one day I have more enemies than after nine years of school in the City? And that's including the mashed potato incident in fifth grade and the BeefSteak incident in eighth. I try to put on my tough face, but it probably looks more like my vaguely ill face. I look over at the girl with the rhinestone glasses, but she's busy drawing something in her sketchbook.

Miss Beans is still talking about learning objectives and methodology, which tells me that she isn't just new here, she's new at teaching, because she hasn't figured out that kids don't care about that stuff. As she's talking, I try to distract myself from the nasty looks I'm getting from across the room. I wonder if all the teachers at this school are named for food. Madame Framboise's name means "raspberry," which I know from the French jam my mother always buys. Then for math there was Miss Mellon. . . .

Just as I'm about to make another one of my life observations, *he* walks in. He hands a note to Miss Beans. He glances around the room while she reads it. He looks in my direction and I smile, hoping he's looking at me and not someone just past my shoulder, some willowy blonde with perfect teeth. But he seems to be looking through me. I start thinking that maybe I was wrong, that this isn't the guy from the beach. I stare down at my desk, feeling my cheeks get hot. Miss Beans finishes the note and scribbles something on it before handing it back to *him*. He looks at me again, and then he's gone.

As the door shuts, the back table starts up again, and I hear words like "cute" float toward me before Miss Beans calls for quiet. I take a peek at the back table again. This time Charity is looking at me. She glares at me for a moment, then mouths, *"Mine."* I turn back to the syllabus on my desk, realizing that somehow I've stepped in it again with her. I scan the words on the page, wondering if in between the list of weekly assignments and the list of topics for the research paper, maybe I'll find a clue about how to get myself out of this mess.

At lunch, instead of sitting alone in the lunchroom or trying to find a small bit of grass to myself out on the lawn, I decide to find my locker. I slide the blue sheet out of my pocket. 311. It's at the end of the next hall. I notice the two girls from my French class whispering together near the water fountain, but I walk past them. *Just ignore them,* I tell myself, but it's hard. I feel my face heating up again. I stop in front of my locker. At least it's a top one. I try the combination, but it won't open. I try it again. Still it won't open. The group near the water fountain has gotten larger. I notice that the bottom part of the locker is bowed out a little and I push it in and hear it click. Maybe that will help. I try it again and this time the latch comes up.

It's another one of those common mistakes people make. The voice inside your head just keeps saying, *I can't believe it. I can't believe it,* even though the evidence is right there. It's the voice that seems to be controlling your muscles, though, because you just stand there, watching. Sometimes the voice in your head changes it up a bit. *"No way." "Nuh uh." "There is no freaking—"* By the time you convince yourself that what you are seeing is real, it's too late. That's how it is with my locker. It starts slowly. One penny falls out. Then two, but then the weight of them pushes the door open and it's a wave of pennies. Hundreds of them. Maybe thousands. A penny tsunami. I mean, how many pennies does it take to fill up a whole locker? And if you've ever poured out a whole jar of change, you know how loud it can be. Now take that noise and multiply it by the number of pennies, the height of the drop from the locker to the floor, and the hardness of the tile in the hallway. If you're thinking car engine gunning or maybe a waterfall, you're close. I keep watching them gush out until it's just a trickle and then done.

"Oh, Pen Knee." I turn and see that the group of girls has grown by one. At the center is Charity. She is smiling that ice smile of hers. "Just our way of saying welcome to Hog's Hollow, Pen Knee," she says. Then all of the girls turn at once and walk away. In fact, most everyone who came running down the hall to see what the commotion was walks away. I guess no one wants to hang around after the prank. I look at the copper sea around me and wonder if I'm supposed to pick all of this up.

"Can you spare some change?"

I turn and see the girl from my art class, the one with the blue-tipped hair, leaning against one of the lockers. She smiles at me.

"Just leave me alone," I say. I shake my Chucks to get the pennies off them.

"You have to hand it to them," the girl says from behind me. "There must be like fifty dollars here." I turn and watch as she bends and fills a hand with pennies then lets them fall back to the floor. The tips of her hair sparkle in the light.

"What do you want?" I ask.

She stands back up and smiles at me. "I'll help," she says.

"Help what?" I have to keep reminding myself not to cry. My eyes keep forgetting.

"Help pick it up. The least you can do is take their money." I turn and face her. "I'm Tally," she says. She tilts her head after she says it and seems to be watching me, waiting to see what I'll do.

"I'm . . ." I look around at the mounds of pennies all over this end of the hall. I look back at Tally and can tell she's trying hard not to laugh, which makes me start smiling. I try again. "I'm Penny," but then I'm laughing and Tally's laughing with me and for one quick moment, I can remember what normal used to feel like.

We empty our backpacks and take turns holding them open and shoveling the mounds of pennies inside. "The way I see it, you're lucky your name wasn't Rotten Egg or something," Tally says.

"Yes, because it would be at this very instant that I would realize what a truly terrible curse the name Rotten Egg is." I scoop the last few handfuls of pennies out of my locker and into my backpack.

"Maybe you led a very sheltered life. I mean, maybe your parents were named Old Gym Sock and Mothball."

We have to leave our backpacks in the office with Constance, who offers us each a Jolly Rancher. We walk back to the main hall, where Tally turns left to go to English and I have to go straight to something called Occupational Investigation.

"Under the clock after school," she says.

"Sure," I say. "I mean, as long as I don't have to be somewhere to embarrass myself in front of the whole school again."

Tally shakes her head and smiles. "It wasn't the whole school."

"Half," I say.

"Maybe half." She's still laughing as she turns to walk down the hall toward her class. It's then that I see the back of her shirt, something that was hidden under the backpack and her hair. RPS FOR PEACE.

chapter five

After school, Tally and I start walking to the bank to change our backpacks full of coins into bills. "I just can't figure out how she got all those pennies," I say. "Even if all of them emptied their coin jars, they couldn't have come up with this many pennies." I shift the straps of my pack slightly to keep them from cutting into my shoulders.

"That part's easy," Tally says. We stop at the corner and wait for a truck pulling a trailer full of pigs to pass. The smell seems to cling to us as we keep walking. "Charlotte's father owns the bank." We cross the street and start up the block toward the bank. The pennies make even the slight hill hard to climb.

"Which one's Charlotte?" I ask.

"Red hair. Pinched face."

"She's in my French class," I say, thinking of the girl in the front row who tried to trip me with her backpack.

"*Oui, oui,*" Tally says.

We walk in silence for the next two blocks. The tiny hill at the end of Main Street makes my heart thud in my chest. I look across the street and see *the guy* from the beach talking to a guy from my math class. The guy from math has a soccer ball in his hands. He keeps dropping it against his knee and catching it as it bounces. The guy from the beach catches the ball and manages to keep it aloft with his knees for almost a minute. It was probably just bad timing, but when he looks in my direction, he knees the ball too hard and sends it into the street. I duck my head and hurry to catch up to Tally, who is now waiting in front of the bank. She holds the door for me, and we go into the lobby. There's a pretty long line in front of the counter.

"So how did they know my locker combination?" I ask.

"One of the Lindseys helps out in the office during first period. You really have to admire how organized they are," Tally says, scooping a tiny bag of pretzels off the New Accounts desk as we pass.

"Yeah," I say, "very admirable."

"I'm just saying"—Tally rips the cellophane bag and takes a pretzel out—"we need to be even *more* organized when we get back at them." I like the way she says *we*. "Let me think about it," she says as she bites into a pretzel.

Lining the walls are old photographs of Hog's Hollow. Most of them are black-and-white, but some are color. There's a photo of an old fishing dock near the end of the town's beach, when it still was a working dock and not just somewhere to hang out. There are pictures of horse-drawn carriages on Main Street and several of women in long dresses with crowns on their heads.

"Hog's Hollow Days," Tally says, looking over my shoulder. She keeps munching away at her pretzels while I walk slowly along the wall. I look at the women in the pictures, their hair-styles hinting at the years when the photos were taken. Bee-hives and sweater sets take up the first row. The second row features photos of girls with impossibly long hair and dresses with lace-up fronts and long skirts. I stop suddenly at one with a girl with blond hair and a long blue dress. Tally almost runs into me. "What?"

"That one," I say, leaning in. "That's my mother." And it's weird how I know it's her. It's not her smile or her hair or her eyes, but the way she was standing with her hands clasped in front of her, one hand holding her other wrist. It's the way she always stands when she's nervous, like she's holding on to her-self to keep herself from floating away.

"Your mother was Miss Hog's Hollow?" Tally asks.

I look at the shiny crown perched crookedly on her head. "I guess," I say, and shrug.

"Around here that is a very big deal."

I look at my mother's face in the photo. I try to see what she was thinking when they took the picture, but after a moment I give up. I can't even figure out what my mom is thinking when she's standing right in front of me.

A man in a three-piece suit walks up to us. "Can I help you girls?" He looks at us as if we smell bad, which we might, after all that walking with heavy backpacks.

"We need to change some money," Tally says. She crunches another pretzel, emptying the tiny bag. He looks at us for a long moment before deciding that stinky or not, we do have money. He directs us over to a teller named Linda. We have to help each other with the backpacks. I put mine on the counter first. It makes a heavy sound followed by a short jingle.

"We'd like to turn these in," I say. Linda lifts the backpack with some effort and upends it over the sorting machine. When most of the coins have filtered through, she takes Tally's. We watch the numbers on the meter flicker past thirty dollars without showing any sign of slowing. Finally the clinking slows to a trickle and then it's silent.

"Seventy-four dollars and ninety-eight cents," Linda says.

"We must have missed a couple," Tally says, winking at me.

Linda takes two pennies from a dish and drops them into the machine. "There," she says, and smiles at us. She counts the bills into my hand. "Next time maybe you shouldn't wait so long." I imagine in Linda's mind we have jars of pennies scattered everywhere.

We take our now empty backpacks and walk outside. I try to hand Tally half of the money, but she won't take it.

"You earned it," she says, smiling. "Just buy me something to eat. I'm starving." She was about to grab another bag of pretzels, but Mr. Three-Piece Suit shook his head at her.

"Like what?" I ask. I stuff the bills into the front pocket of my jeans. We start walking back down the hill and toward the center of town. I look for *him*, but he's gone. *Just as well,* I think.

"Something sweet," she says. "Something chocolate."

"I know just the place."

"How cool is this?" Tally asks.

We sit near the back of the bakery's kitchen on upended milk crates. Gram laughed when I told her the story about the pennies, but I think seeing me with Tally was what really made her happy. She pulled two of my bug cupcakes out of the case, a ladybug one for Tally and a bee for me.

"Your mom is the Cupcake Queen. Awesome," Tally says. She pulls one of the black licorice antennae off her cupcake and chews it. "Wait a minute. This place opened in the middle of summer. Have you been here the whole time?"

I shift on the milk crate. "I've kind of been hiding out," I say. I focus on my cupcake, not wanting to look up at Tally. It is sort of weird how I've been here for three months and I haven't really met anyone.

"I did the same thing when I came here."

I look up at Tally, who is busy chewing the second antennae, this one still attached to the ladybug's head. "Don't look so surprised," she says. "You aren't the only one who was dragged to Hog's Hollow against her will." She pauses and smiles at me. "At least that's what I'm assuming. Most people wouldn't *choose* to come here." She takes a bite out of the top of the cupcake, sending a shower of red sprinkles onto her lap. "You first," she says through a mouthful of cupcake.

"Why am I here?" I ask. She nods and takes another bite, smiling at me with red teeth. I take a deep breath and tell her about my parents separating, leaving out some parts. It's not like it's a secret, but thinking about it still gives me a stomachache. Tally nods and keeps biting at the top of the cupcake. The icing is almost all gone. "I'm going to move back soon," I say. She just raises her eyebrows at me. "Now you," I say, before she can ask any questions.

"Okay," Tally says. She takes a deep breath and brushes crumbs off her lap. "My mom took off when I was small, so it's always been just me and my dad. We moved around a lot. Too much, I guess. My dad's a musician, so we spent a lot of time on the road. So, last winter he decides I need more stability. So now I'm staying with Poppy, my mom's sister. But my dad's coming back to get me soon. As soon as things even out for him." She says it fast, all in one breath, and then looks down in her lap again, suddenly intent on a tiny hole in the knee of her jeans.

Something about the way she's trying to push her baby finger through the hole gives me the feeling I'm not the only one leaving things out. Tally looks up, giving me another half smile before taking another bite of her cupcake. "So, you haven't met anyone else here?" I think about telling her about the guy on the beach, but decide not to when I realize I know more about his dog than about him. I just shake my head. Tally looks at me like she's going to say something else, but she takes the last bite of her cupcake instead.

"What's the RPS Society?" I ask, reading her shirt.

"Rock, Paper, Scissors," she says. "Don't laugh. Some people take it very seriously."

The back door opens. It's one of the deliverymen from the dairy.

"Hey, Mr. Fish," Tally says. Now it seems that *everyone* in Hog's Hollow has a food name. "You're working at the dairy?"

"Hey yourself, Miss Tally. Just making a little extra money. What are you doing here?" He notices me sitting across from her and smiles. "I see someone has found the ghost girl."

"Are you the ghost girl?" Tally asks me. I shrug.

"She's been haunting this bakery all summer," Mr. Fish says, taking off his hat and wiping his forehead with his sleeve. "I was beginning to think maybe only I could see her."

"Nah," Tally says, smiling at me. "She's real enough."

Mr. Fish starts putting the quarts of cream and the boxes of butter into the refrigerator. "How's Poppy?" Mr. Fish asks.

His head disappears behind the door of the refrigerator as he reaches way into the back.

"She's good," Tally says.

He nods. "You tell Poppy I asked about her, won't you?"

"I will," Tally says. Mr. Fish smiles slightly, but his eyes stay sad. He stacks the empty milk crates on top of one another, letting us keep the two we're sitting on. He slips the dolly under the rest and tips the stack toward him.

"See you," he says to us, pushing the screen door open. He leaves, letting the door smack shut behind him.

"That was the infamous Mr. Fish," Tally says, leaning back and brushing at her jeans again. I start to ask why he's infamous, but before I can, she's on her feet. "Okay, then. Friday after school. My house."

I stand and follow Tally to the back door. She shoulders her backpack and pushes the door open.

"Your house?" I ask.

"Big blue house at the end of the beach. Just past the pier." She pushes through the screen door, and I catch it before it slams shut. I watch her walk to the end of the alley and start around the corner. "Friday," she calls.

"Friday," I say, and let the door shut. I turn and see Gram watching me, smiling. "What?" I ask.

"Oh, nothing," Gram says. She walks to the refrigerator and pulls out a sheet pan full of cupcakes. "Any new ideas?" she asks.

"Maybe," I say. "I don't want to tell you in case I can't do it."

"You, Penny, are just like your mother. You can do anything you put your mind to."

The *just like your mother* thing makes me pause for a second. It seems the longer we're in Hog's Hollow, the less certain I am about anything. Most of all my mother.

I sit on the stool in the kitchen and pull out my spiral notebook and pencil. I flip past the designs I made for July (flags and Uncle Sam hats and fireworks). I keep flipping through August. (Sea stars, fishing boats, crabs, beach umbrellas. I even made cupcakes that looked like ice creams. They were huge and baked in real cones.) I had started on September, mostly apples and stacks of books, but I flip to a new sheet of paper and start sketching.

I love art, but I'm not really what you'd call an artist. I mean, I like to do a lot of crafts, and I have a pretty good eye for detail and design, but I can't really do things like the artists who used to have shows in my mom's gallery. Those were all *important* works of art. I'd rather do things that are fun and make people smile than things that make people fold their arms and say "hmmm" a lot. My dad always called it "the art gallery moan," like people were responding at such an emotional level that words couldn't quite capture it.

I take a measuring cup off the hook in front of me and use it to outline a circle on the sheet of paper. I agreed to work here because Gram said if I didn't stop moping around the house, she'd find me a job. It was pretty much *choose* to work at the bakery or get *forced* to work at the boatyard, scraping the underside of the fishing boats, or at Gram's friend's farm, moving compost around. Easy choice. Bakery. At first I just did dishes and stacked supplies and stuff, but then one day my mother got a big order from one of the bed-and-breakfasts, and she needed help. I found out I liked baking and, even more, I liked decorating. Of course I didn't tell Gram that. She's impossible when she knows she's right.

"Hey there," my mother says, coming through the back door. She's wearing jeans with the cuffs rolled up and a tie-dyed T-shirt I've never seen before. She walks behind me and tries to peer over my shoulder. "Can I see?"

"Not yet," I say, putting my hand over my drawing.

My mother turns, reaches into the refrigerator, and takes out a bottle of water. "How was your day?" she asks. I think about French class and Tally and the boy with the dog, who didn't have the dog this time. And about pennies and Rock, Paper, Scissors and the infamous Mr. Fish. And the seventy-five dollars I have stashed in the front pocket of my jeans. I shrug. "The first day can be pretty hard," she says.

"Yeah," I mumble. Like she has any idea. "It was okay, I guess." And I guess that's about right. It was okay.

"Good," she says, and I look back down at my notebook. I try to think if OKAY is an acronym for something. I write

"Ordinary" for the *O* and "Average" for the *A,* but I can't think of anything for the *K* and the *Y.* All I come up with is "Kinda" and "Yellow," but that doesn't make any sense. I sigh and try drawing again. I'll bet Charity didn't know she'd inspire a new cupcake with her locker prank. I have to work carefully on the proportions. Abraham Lincoln has a really long face.

chapter six

So far I have had to change my shirt three times, and that was even before breakfast was over. Shirt number one got splattered when I tried to open the new jar of raspberry jam and ended up wearing half of it. I dumped a mug full of tea on shirt number two. I changed the last time because I found a hole under the arm of my favorite thermal shirt, the one with pictures of sushi all over it.

"Another big day," my mother sings, coming into the kitchen. She's picked up this annoying habit of half singing everything, as if at any moment she's going to burst into song. And the weird thing is, she does it whether she's happy or mad or sad or whatever. It's supremely irritating. She pours herself a cup of coffee and leans against the counter, scrutinizing me. "Is that what you're wearing?" she asks. I look down at my shirt, reading KISS ME. I'M IRISH. Upside down. It's written in fuzzy green print that's starting to peel off from so many washings.

"Yep," I say. I think about singing a response but don't because I'm not sure if she will like it or hate it, and right now I'm not in the mood to be very likable. My mother makes a *humph* sound and then walks to the end of the living room where the computer is set up. I stare out the window, trying to see through the last of the morning fog.

Every night this week I've gone walking on the beach. I tell my mom it's for the exercise. I tell Gram it's because I'm enjoying nature. I tell myself that it's no big deal. I've seen *him* twice, but both times it was from inside my house. Once when we were eating dinner. We'd just sat down. I couldn't figure out how to gobble down a whole bowl of soup and race out the door without drawing a lot of unwanted questions. The other time it was raining, so hard that I thought for sure he wouldn't be out there. But from my dry spot on the glider, I could see two shapes making their way down the beach, one on two legs, the other on four. They were past so quickly that there wasn't any time to get down to the beach. That and because I don't run, there was really no good reason for me to be down there. Well, none I want to admit to.

We're starting with collages in art. We're supposed to bring in "items of personal significance" for our project. We're supposed to express who we are inside. "I want to really see what's going on in there," Miss Beans told us. It's just another example of why I'm pretty sure she's a new teacher. She hasn't figured out that one of the greatest desires that most teenagers have is to *hide* what's going on inside, not collect it all together and glue it onto a big piece of poster board and then hang it out in the hall for just anyone to look at.

"This is lame," I whisper to Tally. Her project is a bunch of liners for CDs and a couple of guitar picks and set lists. I didn't know what those were until she told me it was just a list of the order of songs that a band plays at a gig. She actually talks like that. *A gig.* So really her project isn't about her at all, but about her dad.

"It's pretty summer-campish," she says. I look at my own project and sigh. Mine has a brochure from one of my mom's art shows, some pictures of me and my friends ice-skating in Central Park, and a bunch of ticket stubs from museums and movies. While Tally's project is mostly about when she was on tour with her dad, mine is mostly about my other life, my real life. I try rearranging some of the ticket stubs so they look like they're petals blooming out of the coffee stirrer from Dean & Deluca, but I can't seem to get what Miss Beans calls "layering." I check the clock. Only twelve-fifteen. I'm not sure I can rearrange for fifteen more minutes.

"Penny," Miss Beans says, walking up behind me. I'm busted. I turn and see she's looking at me, not my project. "You look like you could use a break." Okay, so maybe she's not totally clueless. "Could you take this to the office for me?" I nod and she hands me a thick envelope.

"Lucky," Tally hisses at me.

I walk out of the art room and into the empty hall. I stop by the water fountain and get a drink. I'm in no hurry to get back to class. I just can't seem to make the leap between craft and art that Miss Beans talked about. She said the difference is that crafts show the artist's skill while art shows the artist's soul. Whenever I think of my soul, all I picture is a blobby floating thing that changes color depending on my mood.

The office is empty when I walk in. I peer into Constance's bowl of Jolly Ranchers, but all that's left are a couple of sour apple ones and a few blue ones that I guess are raspberry. It's weird how one day someone just decided that blue things were going to be raspberry. Why not blueberry, or plum or something? I look around to see if anyone's watching and reach in for a blue one. The door to the office opens behind me. I drop the candy and turn around, expecting to see Constance walking in, but it's not her.

It's him.

"Caught you," he says with a smile. He comes over, peers into the bowl, then shakes his head. "It's sad really," he says. "I'm pretty sure those are the same candies that are always left." He walks around the desk, opens the middle drawer of the file cabinet, and pulls out the biggest bag of candy I have ever seen. He upends it over the fishbowl, filling it all the way to the top with Jolly Ranchers. He raises his eyebrows and tilts the bowl in my direction. I reach out to take a candy. "The flavor you pick says a lot about a person."

"You've given this a lot of thought," I say.

"That's pretty much my life during third period. Running errands. Developing candy-based theories about people's personalities."

Suddenly, picking a flavor seems to hold a lot of weight. I decide on grape, my favorite.

"Interesting," he says. He puts the bag of candy back in the file cabinet and turns to watch as I unwrap the Jolly Rancher and put it in my mouth.

"So, what's your theory?" I ask.

"It's complicated," he says. "I'll give you the short version for now." I like the way he says "for now." It hints that there is a "later" out there somewhere. "Grape people are artistic and like to be alone a lot."

"What about cherry?" I ask.

"Cherry people are nice." He says "nice" like I'd say "boring."

"I almost picked raspberry," I say.

"Interesting," he says, nodding. "Raspberry people are adventurous. Risk takers." I'm not sure that's me at all.

"What about the others?" I ask.

"Watermelon people are popular." He digs in the bowl, pulling out each flavor as he talks about it. "Apple people try too hard." He pulls out a yellow one and looks at it.

"How about lemon?" I ask.

"Lemon people are mean," he says. "You don't want to get on the bad side of a lemon person." Something tells me Charity is a lemon and the advice is coming too late.

The door opens behind me and I turn to see Constance walk in. I feel myself blush, like I've been caught doing something wrong.

"I have a—I mean, Miss Beans asked me—" I finally just stop talking and hold out the envelope. She takes it and walks around to the other side of the desk, opening it as she goes.

"Thank you," she says, looking up at me. "You can go back to class, um—" She pauses, searching my face.

"Penny," I say. She nods and looks back at her desk. I glance over at *him*, but he's looking at something Constance is handing him. At least now he knows my name.

I head back to class, sucking on the candy. I'm halfway down the hall when the bell rings. Doors open on both sides of me, and soon the hall is completely filled with people opening lockers and grabbing lunches to take outside or to the cafeteria. I thread my way back to the art room and find it empty. My collage is no longer on my desk but scattered under it. There's a big footprint in the middle of my paper. Two of my photos are bent in half, and several of them seem to be missing altogether. I start picking everything up.

"Hey," Tally says from the doorway. "Where have you—" She stops when she sees what I'm doing. She comes over and bends down beside me. "I'm sorry. I just went to get my lunch. I was going to put your collage away, but Miss Beans . . ." She pauses and looks around. "She *was* in here. I wonder where she went."

The snarky part of me thinks *who cares where she went*, but I know it's not Tally I'm mad at and definitely not Tally I should lash out at, so I just keep picking up the pieces of my project and trying to flatten the bent photos.

"Penny," Miss Beans says, walking into the room. "I thought you got lost." She's smiling when she says it. She walks over to where Tally and I are crouched. "Oh, did someone accidentally knock your project off the table?" I nod at the "knock" part. Not the "accidentally" part. "I'm sorry," she says. "I had to go and help a student." She picks up the big piece of poster board. "Charity was having a hard time getting into her locker." I nod. I'm sure she was. More like she was creating a distraction while one of her friends wrecked my project. Miss Beans sees the footprint in the middle of the paper and looks at my face for the first time. "I have more paper, Penny," she says.

I just shake my head, not trusting my voice. I feel like recently everything is either really good or really bad. Mostly really bad.

chapter seven

*I*f someone found out they only had one day to live, they should totally move to Hog's Hollow, because here every day feels like an eternity. So, three eternities later and finally it's Friday. And the only thing I can think to be happy about is that I actually have something to do that doesn't involve butter, sugar, or heavy cream. Today's the day I'm supposed to go over to Tally's house.

I decide to walk there along the beach instead of along the road. I tell myself that it is because it's a nice day and walking along the water is better than along asphalt, but it's not really a nice day. It's raining and the wind is whipping across the water and I have to duck my head to keep the blowing sand out of my eyes. So, exactly what is the reason? Because I'm looking for a big golden dog named Sam. And truthfully not so much the dog, but the guy with the dog.

I climb up the warped wooden steps onto Tally's back porch. Before I reach the door, it opens. "Hi," a woman with curly red hair says. "Come in out of the wet." I try to shake off as much sand and water as I can before entering. Even the inside of my mouth feels gritty. "You must be Penny," she says, smiling. "I'm Poppy. Tally's aunt." She twists a blue ring on her left hand as she talks. "They're in the living room," she says, pointing the way. Then she steps outside. "Tell Tally I'll be in my studio if you guys need anything."

"Thanks," I say. Then it registers. She said *they*. I keep telling myself I'm from Manhattan and this is Hicksville and I should be able to handle meeting new people, but my stomach keeps flipping over. I pass four cats sunning themselves on the windowsill. Each is fatter than the last.

"Yay," Tally says, standing up and walking over to me. "Right on time." She pulls me toward a boy with brown spikes of hair sticking up everywhere. He's bent over two pieces of paper on the floor. "We need someone to break the tie," she says. Okay, when Tally told me "some people" took Rock, Paper, Scissors very seriously, I didn't know she meant *she* does. Or rather *they* do. On the floor are two drawings. One simply says CHOOSE WISELY above a sketch of three hands, one making the sign for a rock, one a pair of scissors, and the other a piece of paper. The other drawing says: PAPER IS THE NEW ROCK.

"They're for our fund-raiser," the guy says. When he talks, the spikes move a little, making him look like a palm tree in the wind.

"Fund-raiser?" I ask.

"For the ARK."

"The ARK?" I'm starting to feel like a parrot.

"Yeah, *R-P-S* for the *A-R-K*," Tally says, saying each letter separately.

"ASAP," Blake says.

"*H-U-S-H,*" Tally says. She turns to me. "The ARK is the animal shelter on the other side of town. We're selling T-shirts to raise some money," I nod, feeling *D-U-M-B*.

"So which one do *you* like, Penny?" Both of them are looking at me. Talk about high pressure. I look from one drawing to the other, then at the two of them waiting.

I get down on my knees and look closer. "Can I have a piece of that?" I ask, pointing to the pad of paper. "And a pencil." I hunch over the pad and sketch quickly. I pause when a cat comes over and bats at the end of the pencil. I'm pretty sure this is a different one—cat number five. When I'm finished, I've combined the two shirts into one. On the front it simply says PAPER IS THE NEW ROCK. On the back are the graphics and the warning to choose wisely. Below that in big letters I've written SAVE THE ARK. I sit back on my heels to let them see.

"Cool," Tally says. "See, I told you." She elbows the guy in the ribs, making his spikes wobble more.

"I'm Blake," he says finally. "Welcome to the Save the ARK Society."

"There are usually more of us—" Tally stops when she sees my questioning face. "Really," she says. "It's the rain. Or maybe it's because school just started."

"Tal," Blake says, leaning back over the pad of paper for a closer look, "it's not the weather. Or school starting." Tally frowns. Blake turns to me. "Tally is in denial."

"I am not," Tally says, folding her arms.

"You're denying you're in denial?" he asks. She squinches up her nose at him. "Everyone is over at the library for the Hog's Hollow Days meeting," Blake says.

Tally is still frowning. "Not everyone," she says.

"Okay," Blake says, smiling at Tally. "*Most* everyone." He turns to me. "It's a very big deal around here." Tally shrugs. "You didn't tell her?" Blake asks, turning to Tally.

She shakes her head. "I do have other things to talk about," she says. She keeps her arms folded and continues to frown, but I can see she's having a hard time keeping up the mad thing.

"Tally was banned from Hog's Hollow Days." He smiles as he says it. I notice Tally lost her battle and is smiling, too.

"How does one get banned?" I ask.

"Tally and the events coordinator had creative differences."

I lift my eyebrows at her. She shrugs again. "Long story. Let's just say I could have handled it better," she says. Blake shakes his head. "You hungry?" she asks. I guess I'm not going to get the whole story now.

"Starved," I say, and follow them into the kitchen. We stand around the island, munching on apples and oatmeal cookies. I count six cats now. Blake turns on the radio. "I love this song," I say. Tally bites into her apple.

"You like Nathan's Sunday?" Blake asks.

"Like them? Doesn't everyone?" I ask. He nods and smiles. "I tried to get tickets when they played Madison Square Garden."

"No luck?" Blake asks.

"No. I mean, maybe if my mom had let me camp out over-night." That was a huge argument between Mom and me. One that lasted for weeks. It's funny—I used to really stand up to her on things. But moving to Hog's Hollow has changed that somehow. Now I can't even stand up to her when she wants to buy Super Chunk Skippy instead of the smooth Jif that I like.

Blake reaches for another cookie and I turn and gaze out at the ocean. The whole back wall of the kitchen is windows, so you can see a wide length of the beach. The sun is fighting through the clouds, brightening the sky. Hanging in front of the window are dozens of glass balls, each swirled with color.

"They're Poppy's," Tally says, seeing me looking at them.

"She made those?" I ask. Tally nods. I walk over and reach up to touch one of the balls gently. It spins slowly, casting rain-bows of light all over the room.

I hear a door slam and soon Poppy enters the kitchen. She pulls a handkerchief from her head, letting her red hair spill across her forehead.

"You found the cookies," Poppy says. She takes one of the apples and bites into it. She reaches down and rubs an orange cat behind the ears.

"These are amazing," I say, touching a ball covered in spirals of blues and greens. "It looks like the ocean." Poppy leans against the counter, watching me. I walk along the window, examining all of them, but I'm drawn back to the first one, the ocean one. I touch it again, watching the waves of blue and green shift as it spins gently. I always feel like I'm not going to say the right thing about someone's art, like I don't know the right words. "They are really beautiful," I say.

Poppy smiles and says, "Thank you," and I feel like maybe I did say the right thing. Is it that easy—just say what you think?

"Oh," Tally says through a mouthful of cookie, "I saw Mr. Fish the other day."

Poppy looks at Tally. "I haven't seen him in a long time." She takes another bite of apple and chews thoughtfully. "Not really since he moved."

"He seemed good," Tally says. "He's working at the dairy."

"If you see him again . . ." Poppy stops and looks at the apple in her hand. "I was going to tell you to ask him to drop by." Tally nods, and they look at each other for a moment. "Maybe I'll swing by the dairy and just say hi."

Poppy smiles at me. "Penny, feel free to come over anytime. You seem to have a real eye for art." She picks up the handkerchief and ties it over her hair again. "Of course I mean that in a very self-congratulatory way." She laughs at herself. "You'll have to excuse me. I have a date with a soldering iron." She lobs the apple core at the trash can as she walks toward the window. "The rain's stopped. You should go out." She smiles over at Tally. "You know, fresh air and all that."

Tally rolls her eyes, making Poppy laugh again.

"I am always up for a walk on the beach," Blake says. I nod, feeling a little flutter in my stomach. *Quiet,* I tell it. I can't be all fluttery over some boy I've only just met.

We head out, pulling on jackets and sweatshirts against the mist that the rain left behind. We walk along in silence for a while. Tally seems lost in thought and Blake is munching on the two cookies he swiped before heading out the door. We step over a long swath of seaweed and pass a cluster of seagulls that seem overly territorial when we get too close to their pile of rocks.

"Listen," Tally says, stopping and taking my arm. "Do you trust me?"

"I, uh . . ." I'm not sure how to answer her question. Luckily Blake does.

"Tal, she just met you. All she knows about you is that you committed some sort of crime serious enough to get you banned from a wholesome community event, and you are obsessed with items you can find in office supply stores or here on the beach."

"You can't find scissors on the beach."

"You know what I mean," Blake says.

"Okay," Tally says, turning back to me. "I'll rephrase. Do you trust me enough to let me spearhead your revenge on Charity?"

I hadn't really been thinking revenge. More like truce.

It's as if Tally can read my thoughts. "You can't just let them get away with it," she says.

I look at Blake, and he shrugs, leaving it up to me.

"Okay," I say. "What's your plan?"

"The fewer people who know about it, the better," she says. I wait, but she doesn't say anything else. I almost ask again, but then I think about Tally's question: Do I trust her? And I decide I do, because that's what trust is—a decision.

"Can we get a hint?" Blake asks.

"Let's just say that when it's over, Charity will have suffered a blow and she will have no one to blame but herself."

"Sweet," Blake says. "What can we do?" Again there's that word *we* I've come to like so much.

"I am going to need a little petty cash," she says.

I think of the seventy-five dollars I have stuffed into my Tootsie Roll bank. "Done," I say.

She smiles. "Okay, then." She turns and walks quickly down the beach. As Blake and I follow behind, Blake tells me who owns each house we pass. He seems to have a story about every family.

"Do you know everyone in Hog's Hollow?" I say.

He shrugs and bites into his last cookie. "I've lived here all my life," he says. "In small towns, knowing things about other people is like breathing. You can't help it, even if you wanted to." We walk a little farther, stepping across another big piece of seaweed that was dragged up in the last storm. "That's the Cathance place." I look up at a house with purple pansies spilling off the back porch. "He's a botanist," he says. "Orchids mostly," he says. "He's trying to create a new kind. He wrote out a whole explanation for me if you want to read it."

"You never know when you're going to need detailed orchid information," I say, making Blake smile.

Another house comes into view, but this one is closed up, its back door boarded over. We keep walking and I wait for the story, but Blake is quiet.

"How about that one?" I ask.

"The Fishes," he says.

"As in Mr. Fish?" I ask.

He nods. Tally has stopped and is looking out over the water. We stop and stand with her.

"Why is it all boarded up?" I ask.

"About a year and a half ago, there was an accident." Blake nods toward the distant islands. "Out there." Blake looks back at me. "It was pretty bad."

"An accident?" I ask.

"His wife went out by herself in a kayak. A freak storm hit. The divers from the state police were all over the bay, searching. They finally found parts of the boat and then they found her." Blake looks back out at the water. "Like I said, it was pretty bad." I nod, not knowing what to say.

Tally picks up the story. "Mr. Fish kind of went nuts. He used to just walk the beach. Up and down, for hours." She looks over at me. "Poppy used to come out with food for him. On nights when I couldn't sleep, I'd go out on the porch and he'd still be out there. Just walking." Tally kicks a piece of driftwood, scaring some seagulls that were cracking mussels against the rocks. "Sometimes I would see his son out here with him, all bundled up against the cold. Then one day, they were gone. They just boarded up the house and moved into town."

"That was the last time Mr. Fish has ever set foot on the beach," Blake says. He picks up half of a mussel shell and throws it into the water. It floats for a moment, like a tiny boat, until a wave hits it and it disappears.

"So, he's better now?" I ask.

"Define *better*," Tally says, looking at me out of the corner of her eyes.

That's a tough one. I'm not sure I can. Luckily Tally lets me off the hook. "Now he spends most of his time out in the woods." She waves her hand toward the hills above town.

"Doing what?" I ask.

"Some kind of project," she says. "There are all kinds of theories—"

"Like I was saying about small towns . . ." interjects Blake.

"—but no one knows for sure." Tally talks over him.

"What happened to Mr. Fish's son?" I ask.

"He's around." Tally pauses, looking up at a gull circling above us. "Sort of. For a while it seemed like he was out of school more than he was in it. He was always ditching and taking off. He started volunteering at the ARK around the time I did, some sort of community service thing to keep him from get-ting suspended." Tally shades her eyes against the sun that's just peeking through the clouds. "That's where he got his dog," she says. "Since then, he seems better. Happier."

"The dog?" I ask, feeling the flip-flop. I tell it to hush. There are a bazillion dogs in the world.

"He is awesome," Tally says. Blake looks at her, making her smile. "I meant the dog!"

"Uh-huh," Blake says. "I see how all you girls are around that guy." Blake makes his voice go all high. "Ohhh, he's sooo cute."

Tally punches him lightly in the arm. "He's got nothing on you, Pineapple Head." Blake starts blushing like crazy. Tally turns to me. "However, Marcus *is* cute. Messed up, but cute. You've probably seen him. Just before dark, running on the beach. Just him and his dog, Sam."

chapter eight

*J*ust in case you don't know, you should never, ever say the following: "Well, I guess it can't get any worse." Because here's the lesson that I learned today: it can.

I'm sitting in art, spreading gesso over my canvas. Miss Beans is going around the room, watching. She's different from the art teachers I had in the City. There it was all art theory and "finding your inner muse." Miss Beans is all about technique. "Art, like anything else, requires practice," she says. I'm trying to paint in long, smooth strokes, so you can't see my brush marks, but it's hard. I keep overlapping the last pass and leaving these little ridges.

The door opens and there he is again, but this time I know his name: Marcus. He has to pass right by where I'm sitting to get to the teacher. *Ignore him.* My brain is trying to stay on task, but my hand seems to have a mind of its own. My next pass is so wiggly that it looks like a wave is breaking right in the middle of my canvas. I peek at the front of the room, where Marcus is handing an envelope to Miss Beans. I will him to look my way, but he doesn't. He waits while Miss Beans writes something on a piece of paper then folds it and gives it back to him. He turns, making me duck. *Calm down.* My next pass of the brush is even worse. The pileup of gesso is starting to look more mountain range-ish and less wave-ish. I keep my head down as Marcus walks toward me. He slows as he gets close. His hand hovers over the corner of my desk and then he's past and out the door before I can register what's happened. The grape Jolly Rancher sitting on my desk is the only evidence that he was here. I fold my hand over the candy and pull it into my lap before anyone can see.

"Miss Beans." I glance up to see one of the girls at the back table, one of the Lindseys (yes, there are three of them), waving her hand. She asks something about her canvas. Charity gets up and starts making her way across the room. I look back down at my work. *If I mind my own business, they'll leave me alone.* I try to brush out the ridges by going across them as Miss Beans showed us. I start on another ridge, happy that I'm finally starting to figure out something.

That feeling lasts about seven seconds.

I hear it first, then feel it. The tub of gesso that I'm using is upended on my table and the paint slowly spills into my lap. Charity stands in front of me, watching, waiting to see what

I'll do. What I do is just sit there. She smiles slightly and continues toward the supply closet.

"Oh, Pen Knee," one of the Lindseys says from the back table. "What happened?"

Miss Beans turns and looks at me, first at my face and then at the pool of gesso spreading under my feet. I stand up, watching it roll down my legs. Unfortunately, Tally is in the library picking up some art books for Miss Beans, so I'm alone in my soggy mess. Miss Beans walks over and hands me a stack of paper towels, which I use to try to mop up the front of my jeans. Charity is standing by the supply closet, smirking. I feel the heat behind my eyes. I have to blink fast to make the tears stay inside. The only thing worse than their seeing me with paint all over is their seeing me cry about it.

"Start cleaning up, class," Miss Beans says. She watches the back table as they put tops on their tubs of paint and stack their canvases on the drying rack. I keep wiping my chair and then the floor—anything to keep my face hidden. I know my eyes are red. I've always admired girls who can cry prettily, all shiny eyes and flushed cheeks. With me it looks like I have just had a terrible reaction to a bee sting. My eyes get all red and puffy and my nose starts running like mad.

The bell rings and everyone heads out for lunch. I hear a burst of laughter from the Lindseys and their leader once they hit the hall.

Miss Beans walks over to me and I concentrate on her paint-splattered clogs. "Want to tell me what happened?" I shake my head and stand up. "Come on into my office," she says. I follow her, trying to ignore the squishing in my sneakers.

She stops at her desk and looks at me for a moment before leaning down to pull out a cardboard box. Inside is a big mound of clothes. "Take whatever you want," she says. "I've learned to expect accidents in art class." The way she says "accidents" lets me know that she knows it wasn't really an accident. She leaves the office and closes the door behind her so I can get changed. I peel my still damp jeans off my legs and try to wipe away the goo that seeped through them. I just want to be away from here. I want to be back in my old life, where no one dumped paint on me and where the best thing going isn't some Hog festival and where people like Charity and the Lindseys would be eaten for lunch.

"Is Penny still here?" I recognize Tally's voice out in the classroom.

"She's just getting changed," Miss Beans says.

I rifle through the box until I find a pair of jeans that might work. They're too big, but I find a scarf and slip it through the belt loops. I stuff my socks and jeans into a plastic bag I find in another box under Miss Beans's desk. I have to pull my still damp shoes on, but at least my legs are mostly dry. I blow my nose and blot at my eyes, trying to catch the blue mascara before it streaks my face.

"Nice," Tally says as I open the door. "Very bohemian."

I smile slightly and walk to my table. I keep my head down, trying to make my hair hide my face. I pick up a paper towel and bend to wipe the gesso that splashed up the legs of my chair, but Miss Beans stops me.

"Go have lunch, Penny," she says. "I'll get it."

"Thanks," I say, picking up my notebook. Tally and I walk over to my new locker. After the penny incident, I asked to switch. I pull out my lunch. The idea of eating nauseates me, but I feel like if I don't do the next thing, I'm going to really start crying or screaming or something.

"Let's go where we can talk," Tally says. Instead of going to the front lawn like most everyone else, Tally leads me to the wall outside of the library.

"Tell me," Tally says. I just shake my head. "Charity?" she asks, and I nod. She sighs and looks away.

"I hate it here," I say. Tally looks down at her sandwich. "I just want to be away from here, from all of—" I pause and look at my hands. What I'm saying must hurt Tally's feelings some, but I can't stop. "I just want to go home," I say, and this last bit makes me start crying again because I realize I don't really have one anymore. Tally hands me a paper towel from her lunch bag and I blow my nose hard. When I do, it makes a honking sound. "I'm a mess," I say.

"A little."

"A lot." I blow my nose again, making sure there's no honk this time. "It just stinks, you know?"

Tally looks past me for a moment. "I know," she says, and something about the way she says it makes it seem like she does. She reaches into her lunch sack and pulls out a Ziploc of gummy cherries and hands it to me. "They'll make you feel better," she says. I bite the stem off of one. "Better?" she asks.

"A little. Thanks."

Tally smiles her lopsided smile. "I told Blake about your mom being on the wall at the bank. Remember how he says he knows everything about this place?"

I just nod, chewing the rest of the gummy.

"Well, his mom told him something about your mom. Turns out she beat Charity's mom for the title of Hog Queen not just that one year, but all four years they were in high school."

I keep chewing the gummy until it doesn't taste like much of anything anymore.

"What I'm trying to tell you is that it's not just what happened at Charity's party."

"Great." *Thanks for the heads-up, Mom.*

Tally crumples her lunch bag and lobs it into the trash can.

"So what's the big deal about being Hog Queen?" I ask.

Tally shrugs. "The appeal is lost on me. I mean, getting the sash and the crown and getting to ride on the float shaped like a hog's head is awesome for sure."

"You're joking." I'm trying to picture my mother in her long dress with a sash around her and a sparkling tiara on her head, waving from a float towed behind an old farm truck.

"Wait, it's better than that. You also get to keep the genuine crystal bust of a hog in your house."

"I didn't even know a hog had a bust," I say.

Tally giggles. "You also get a year's supply of bacon and sausage and other pork products from Franklin Farms."

"So does Charity think she's going to be Hog Queen?" I ask.

"I'm sure," Tally says. "If only for the pork products." She kicks her heels against the wall we are sitting on. "What do you know about pigs?" she asks.

"Nothing," I say. By now I'm used to Tally's odd questions.

The bell rings. "You okay?" Tally asks.

I shrug. "I guess. Do I look awful?"

She tilts her head at me. "Not awful," she says, smiling. "Your eyes are just a little red." She stands up and picks up her books. "You ready, or do you need to sit for a while? I can be late."

I shake my head and stand up. I try to hand the rest of the gummies back to Tally, but she says, "Keep 'em. They match your eyes."

"Awesome," I say. "Red eyes are so attractive." Tally elbows me, making me laugh. We head back into the school and toward our lockers. As we walk down the hall, my shoes squish with damp gesso. One of the Lindseys is talking and laughing with Charlotte near my locker.

"Forget about them," Tally says.

My cheeks are burning and my eyes are glued to the floor as

I walk past. If I keep my head down, my hair will cover my face.

"Hey, watch where you're going," a voice says. I look up to see Charity standing in front of me. I mean, *right* in front of me. If I hadn't stopped when I did, I would have run into her. But it's not her I'm looking at, it's who she's talking to. Marcus. He doesn't even look in my direction; instead he seems intent on something beyond my left shoulder. Without acknowledging me, he moves past. I turn and watch him walk over to a group of guys all in varsity soccer uniforms. Charity smirks. "Stare much?" she asks. There's a burst of laughter behind me.

Tally's waiting for me at her locker. She raises her eyebrows at me as I walk over. I shake my head and lean against the row of lockers beside hers, trying to look like I'm not actually looking at what I'm looking at. Marcus is still talking with the soccer players. He takes a ball from one of them and bounces it from one knee to the other before catching it. Then, finally, he looks over to where I'm still trying to seem like I'm not looking. He watches me for a moment and then disappears down the hall, the group of soccer players following.

"That's Marcus," Tally says.

"Yeah," I say, feeling the heat on my face. She keeps watching me, smiling. I try not to meet her eyes. Instead I check out the inside of her locker. Her books are stacked neatly according to size, but that's not what makes me pause. Perched on her book tower is a huge can with a spoon sticking out of the top.

It's one of those cans you find only in Sam's Club or Costco or *maybe* in the Impossibly Big Food aisle of the grocery store. It's the generic brand, with no picture or even any color on its label. It only has one word on it, in huge black print: LARD.

Tally looks around like she's about to do something she doesn't want anyone to see. Once she does it, I know why. She takes the spoon out of the can with a big glop of lard on it and puts it into her mouth. I hear a series of gasps behind me. I don't even have to turn around to know who is standing there watching.

"Have you lost your mind?" I ask. Tally doesn't answer. She just sticks the spoon back in the can and closes her locker. She makes a big production of swallowing, even making a happy noise at the end, like you might hear after the first bite of pumpkin pie at Thanksgiving. I turn and look behind me in time to see Charity and her friends walking away, whispering.

"What was all that about?" I ask. I'm thinking reverse anorexia, weird cravings.

"Trust me," Tally says. She picks up her notebook and starts walking, making me follow. I'm still trying to get my head around the Can of Animal Fat Show, but Tally's already moved on. "So, Marcus," she says. "I told you he runs on the beach around dusk." I just nod. "Okay, then," she says, and smiles.

"Okay what?" Blake asks, walking up to us.

"Nothing," I say. I feel myself blushing again.

"Nothing," Tally says, and she winks at me.

chapter nine

I lean my elbows against the top of the display case and watch people walk past on the sidewalk. I know the only reason my mother asked me to work the front of the bakery this afternoon was because Thursday afternoons are always so slow. That and she didn't have anyone else. Gram is in Lancaster doing a series of portraits for a family. I helped her load her milk crate of snuggle toys into her car before she left. She threw in a couple of puppets and a plastic fishing toy with a clump of feathers glued to the string. "Whatever it takes to get the shot," Gram told me before pushing the back closed and climbing into the car.

Then Mom left about an hour ago with strict instructions not to leave the front unless there was an emergency. I have to fight the urge to put my head down on the counter. I suddenly feel really tired through and through, from the end of my ponytail to the bottoms of my still slightly squishy sneakers. I had no idea gesso could stay damp for so long. I ditched the borrowed jeans for a clean pair at home, but I couldn't find any other shoes. I open the back of the case and start rearranging the cupcakes, sliding them toward the front. The penny cupcakes have been selling pretty well, but the best sellers are still the triple chocolate mud slides. It was hard to make it look like there was an actual mud slide on the top of the cupcakes without them looking gross, like someone got sick on them. I check my phone for about the fortieth time. I left another message on my dad's voice mail. It's starting to get pathetic. Either he's incredibly busy or he just doesn't want to deal with me.

The other person I've been trying to reach is Tally. The whole *can-of-lard-in-the-locker* thing is making me crazy. All Tally does is smile and tell me to trust her. It's just too weird to get my head around. The sleigh bells on the front door jingle, making me look up.

"Hi," I say, sliding the case closed. The UPS delivery guy whose name I can never remember, Paul or Saul, walks in and places a heavy padded envelope on the counter. I read the name on his ID badge. STEVE. Not even close.

He slides his electronic mail tracker out of the holster on his belt. I notice he has a place for his cell phone and a clip for his keys and even a miniflashlight. He's the postal equivalent of Batman. "Where's your mom?" he asks. He taps the digital pen against the screen a few times before putting the unit on the counter in front of me.

"Meeting," I say, signing my name in the tiny box on the screen. I have to do it three times before it resembles anything like my signature. Even then it looks like my name is Pezzy Leme. Steve takes a sample from the tray and pops it into his mouth. I push the pen back into its holder and pick up the envelope. It's soft, but heavy. TALBOTS & TALBOTS, ATTORNEYS-AT-LAW, with a Manhattan address in the corner. It's addressed to my mother. Ms. Elizabeth Lane.

Steve helps himself to another sample before sliding his tracker back into his belt.

"Tell your mom I said 'hi.'" I just nod and keep looking at the envelope. CONFIDENTIAL is stamped on the front in red ink. The bells jingle as the door eases shut behind him. I flip the envelope over and look at the tear strip on the back. There's no way I can sneak it open. I sigh and put it on the counter behind me. It seems like really important things keep happening all around me and no one is talking about them. At least not to me.

I pick up the sample tray and walk back into the kitchen to cut up a couple more cupcakes. I've just finished arranging quarters of cupcakes on the tray when the back door opens. Mom pushes her sunglasses up on top of her head but keeps talking on her cell, frowning at me as she walks past. Even though I'm doing my job, that frown makes me feel like she's caught me slacking. I push the door toward the front open with my hip and walk around the front of the counter. I put down the tray of samples and start brushing up crumbs with my hands. My mother snaps her cell phone shut as she pushes through the door. She stands on the other side of the counter, the frown now trained on everything she sees. I try to look through her eyes. I see a few fingerprints on the display case, way up in the corner, where they missed the sweep of my cloth. I see that the triple chocolate cupcakes are uneven. She sighs and finally looks at me. But it's the same way she's been looking at everything else. Judging, calculating, studying.

"Did anyone come in?" she asks.

"Just the UPS guy." I have to say the list of names in my head again. *Paul. Saul.* "Steve," I say aloud. "He left that." I point to the envelope on the back counter. Mom picks it up and then frowns at it, too. I wait, hoping she'll say something about it, but she doesn't. She takes it into the back and I hear her pulling the strip, ripping the envelope open. I start to follow her, but the bells on the door ring and soon I am boxing up cupcakes for two women in jeans and twin sets, who seem forced-relaxed in a way that tells me they're from the City. As they leave I hear the back door open and then Gram's voice. She starts talking about the family she just photographed. How the baby spit up on the father's suit and the two children started fighting over a toy, which led to a skirt being torn and a black eye. Her voice sounds tired. My mother keeps *um humming,* as though she's barely listening. Then she says something so softly I can't hear it. I stand next to the door to hear better and think, *I've been reduced to eavesdropping.*

"It's a good offer," my mother says. "I should probably take it."

"Have you told Penny?" Gram asks, and I'm nearly leaning against the door. *No!* I want to shout. *No one is telling me anything!*

My mother sighs. "I will," she says. "As soon as it's more definite. I mean, I wouldn't want to tell her and then have to *un*tell her."

"I think you should tell her," Gram says. "But it's your choice."

I hear footsteps coming toward the door. I back up and busy myself with wiping the counter. "Penny," Gram says, pushing through the door. "I have to tell you about the shoot."

"Later," I say, moving past her toward the back. I'm tired of everyone hiding things from me, making decisions behind my back and telling me when it's too late to change anything. "I'm going . . ." I start to say "home," but then I realize I'm not sure where that is anymore. "I'm going back to the house," I say. I pick up my backpack and sling it over my shoulder. I go out into the alley without even pulling on my coat. I can see my mother's face as she looks up from the papers and Gram's as she watches me from the doorway. I just keep walking, head down, feeling the cold seep all the way through me, settling deep inside.

I drop my backpack in the entry hall when I get to Gram's. I kick off my shoes and put them in the washer, where I dropped my jeans and socks earlier. Maybe a good wash will get the slightly moldy gesso smell out of everything. I pull on a pair of sweatpants that are sitting on the dryer and walk into the kitchen. The clock on the oven blinks. Nearly five. I'm on my own for a while. I know Gram and Mom will be late getting home. They have to put together a huge wedding order. I feel a tiny bit bad for not helping, but I just had to get out of there. I pull a sleeve of Saltines out of the pantry and sit on the window seat, looking out at the ocean. I lean my face against the glass. It feels cool against my cheek. I keep thinking the one thing I've been thinking all day. *I just want to go home. I want to go away from this place where everyone either hates me or hides things from me.* I sigh and put the corner of a cracker in my mouth. And then I do a dumb thing. I only say it to myself, but it's enough. *At least it can't get any worse.*

The phone rings, making me jump.

"Hello?" I'm expecting Mom or Gram or maybe Tally. It's not any of them. It's my dad.

"Hey, sweetheart," he says. "I got your message."

I try to think of something to say but can't. Ever since we left the City, there's been this big gap between us that neither of us seems to be able to cross. "Listen," he says finally, "I need to talk to your mother. Is she there?" They only refer to each other as they relate to me now. *Your father. Your mother.*

"She's still at the bakery," I say.

"Oh," he says, and then there's this tiny laugh. "The bakery."

He sounds like he's making quotation marks with his fingers and rolling his eyes. Part of me agrees with him, and part of me gets mad. "Listen, just tell your mom I got the paperwork today." I'm thinking, *What paperwork?* But I don't have to wait long for an answer. "Tell her I talked to the Realtor. If she can get everything filed before the weekend, we can close before the end of the month."

Somewhere in all those unfamiliar terms, I realize he's talking about an apartment. And I get excited. I mean, people who are splitting up don't buy a new apartment together, do they? I'm thinking a great walk-up in SoHo or maybe one of those places in Tribeca that are funky-cool even if they need a lot of work.

But as he keeps talking, I realize that's not what he's saying at all. He's not talking about some new place we're buying, but our old apartment in the Village and how we have a good offer and he thinks it's a good time to sell. He keeps saying "we" and "us," as if I have any say in all of this.

He finally stops. I know he's waiting for me to say something, but I've got nothing. He clears his throat and takes a breath loud enough for me to hear it through the phone. "Penny, I know you've been through a lot, but just remember your mother and I still love you very much." And I wonder if he's reading from *The Big Book of Stupid Things Parents Say to Their Children.*

All of a sudden I feel dizzy and too hot and I'm afraid I'm

going to throw up. But my dad just keeps talking and talking until I have to pull the phone away for a minute so I can breathe.

I hear my name and put the receiver back to my ear. "What?" I ask.

"Penny," my dad says, "did you hear me?"

"Yeah," I say, but it comes out more as a whisper than anything.

"Are you okay, Bean?" he asks. He hasn't called me that in years. I can feel the tears coming again.

"I just hate it here," I say. "I want to come home. I miss you."

"I know, Bean. I miss you, too." He's quiet, and for a moment I wonder if the call dropped, but then he clears his throat. "Listen, I want you to know that you always have a place with me. Just say the word and you can come here," he says.

I want to say "the word," but I don't know what it is. *Help?* Then I realize I don't even know where "here" is. I've never been to his new place. I only know it's somewhere uptown. He starts talking about his apartment building and how it has a rooftop garden and how it's right around the corner from the Museum of Natural History. He keeps adding details, but they're just adding to the sinking feeling in my stomach.

"I mean, just think . . ." he says, and I am, but not about his new apartment and his new kitchen and his new life, but about my old one and how it's going away.

"Listen, Dad," I say. "I have to go, okay?"

"Sure," he says. "Think about it, Penny." There's silence for a moment. "Let's talk—" But I don't hear the rest because I push the *End* button on the phone and drop it onto the window seat.

I try to calm myself by looking at the ocean again, but it's dark out now, and all I can see is my own reflection looking back at me. The sick feeling won't go away. I want to get out of my own skin, but I can't. So I do the next best thing—get out of the house. I pull my windbreaker tight around me and walk down the trail until the water covers my feet. *I can't believe they're selling the apartment.* I know it's just a place, but it's *our* place. "If the apartment goes, what's next?" I ask the seagull sitting on a rock near me. He doesn't answer, just looks at me and flies away. The wind coming off the water makes my teeth chatter, but I just stand there, letting my toes sink into the soft sand. Somehow, with each announcement my parents make, my old life seems to drift farther and farther away. I let the cold water lap against my ankles. And along with the cold, something else begins to seep into me. Like the water pulling at my feet, it threatens to pull me under. It's a feeling of hopelessness. And of being completely alone.

Gram says if you stand on the beach long enough, eventually everything will come to you. I'm sure she was talking about ideas. But while I'm standing there, feeling cold and miserable and sorry for myself, something does come to me. When it does, it knocks me down.

"Oh man, I am so sorry."

I have to squint because my eyes are filled with either sand or salt water or tears—or more likely all three. "Here." I can see well enough to know that a hand is reaching out to help me up. I let myself get pulled back to standing. Now I'm wet all the way through. But it doesn't matter, because I now realize whose hand I was just holding. "I am *so* sorry," he says again, and I feel something soft being pushed into my hands. I use it to wipe at my eyes. I keep the soft thing pressed against my face for a moment, listening to the sound of a dog's soft chuffing and then his panting and the dull thudding of his tail against the sand. "I am so sorry."

I look up and smile. "You already said that." Marcus has one hand on Sam's collar and the other is nervously combing through his hair.

"I *am* sorry. I mean, *we're*—" Sam chuffs again as if in agreement.

"It's okay," I say, first to Marcus and then to Sam. I put my hand out to Sam, who is straining to get to me. I let him lick my hand and I rub him behind the ears. Marcus is only wearing sweatpants and a T-shirt, and I realize that I've been wiping myself with his sweatshirt. "It's just a little water," I say.

"And sand," Marcus says.

"And sand." I'm not as nervous as I was when I saw him in the hallway. Maybe because it's dark, or maybe because I'm soaking wet, or maybe it's because we don't have an audience, or maybe it's just because of Sam. "Thanks for the candy."

Marcus shrugs, and for an instant I wonder if girls all over the school are getting Jolly Ranchers from him. Maybe he just started giving them to me because he needed a new grape girl. Then he smiles at me.

"I'm sorry we interrupted you," Marcus says.

"I was just thinking." Saying it makes the thoughts start up again.

"The beach is a good place for it," he says.

I picture him and his father walking up and down the shore after his mother died. Thinking about his parents makes me think about my own. How they seem only half there, like ghosts. And I imagine what it would be like to lose one of them. Here one day, then gone completely. I can't even get my mind around it. I mean, my dad is busy and my mom is sort of confused, but I still know where they are.

Sam stops straining and sits, as if he's thinking thoughts of his own. He's quiet, except for his tail, which keeps beating the sand. Marcus lets go of his collar, and Sam comes and sits by me, leaning against my leg. He feels warm and solid, which I don't have much of right now. All three of us watch the waves as they push toward shore, breaking into low whitecaps and then drifting across the pebbled beach. As the water pulls back away from us, it rolls across the rocks, dragging them along with it, making a low rumbling sound.

"When I was little I thought that was a monster growling," I say. It's out before I can stop it.

But almost before I finish Marcus says, "Me, too." He looks over at me. "But now it seems more like it's whispering than growling."

I listen for a moment, the waves breaking and the water sliding over the sand. "It does," I say. I like how he changed it for me with just one word. "I wish I could understand what it's saying."

"You mean you don't speak Ocean?" Marcus asks.

"Nope," I say. "Just Spanish, sort of. And *un peu de français.* How about you?"

"Un peu français aussi," he says.

I smile at his affected French accent. "Actually, I meant do you speak Ocean?"

"Oh," Marcus says. "Well, they don't offer Ocean at HHHS. I mean, not officially."

"But unofficially?" I ask, playing along.

"To a select few." He pretends to look serious. "Actually it's a pretty small club. Just two members." I'm starting to think there are a lot of small clubs in Hog's Hollow. "But, we are looking to expand our membership. Are you interested?"

"Definitely," I say. "What do I have to do?"

"You just have to get approval from the rest of the club."

"Oh," I say, nodding.

Marcus bends and pets Sam, who is still leaning against me. "Looks like you have one vote," he says.

"Just one?" I ask.

Marcus looks up at me, and even in the moonlight I can see him blush. He straightens up and gazes back out over the water. "I think it's unanimous," he says. We stand quietly for a bit, just watching the waves and listening to the sounds of the pebbles shifting against one another.

"So what's it saying now?" I ask.

"It's more of a feeling, really. Not words." He's quiet again. The wind is cold against my damp skin, making me shiver, but I stand as still as I can. If I move, even a little, I'm going to ruin this moment. "It's sad tonight." His voice is soft. I wonder if it's always sad for him. And if it is, why does he keep coming out here?

Sam sneezes. The sudden noise startles us. Marcus shifts a little away from me, and it's like the bubble that we made burst.

"We should get home," Marcus says. He smiles slightly. The mouth-only smiling must run in their family because it's the same smile Mr. Fish has. I wonder if that's how it's always been with them or if it's something that crept in after the accident and never left.

I try to think of something to say, but like so many other times recently, I feel like I have nothing and too much in my head at the same time. When I look at him, I realize whatever was between us has vanished. I try to hand him his sweatshirt.

"Keep it," he says. "I'll get it back later." He smiles one more time then starts heading away down the beach. Sam stays beside me, leaning heavily, until he, too, takes off into the night.

His weight against my leg disappears so quickly that I almost fall again. Over the sound of the waves and the shifting pebbles, I imagine I can just make out the sound of sneakers hitting the hard pebbles followed by the nearly silent sound of paws striking the hard sand.

I make my way slowly through the deep sand back up to the house. The house is dark except for the one lamp in the living room that's on a timer. I feel a little like that—cold and dark, with just one small light deep inside. But when I think about Marcus, I feel guilty for feeling so sad about my problems.

I stomp on the mat near the back door, trying to knock off as much sand as I can. I don't bother flipping on any lights. Sometimes with the lights on it feels like I'm even more alone, like I'm on this tiny, lit island in a sea of darkness. I sit back on the window seat, feeling the dampness of my sweatpants seep into my legs. I should change, I think. But I don't. I just keep sitting, listening to the sound of the waves filtering in through the open door. I lift Marcus's sweatshirt up to my face and breathe in. Somehow the strange smells just make me feel like I don't belong here even more than before. I keep breathing in, trying to find something familiar, but it just smells salty and musty and slightly of wet dog.

chapter ten

My eyes all puffy from all the crying. It feels like they are permanently sealed shut. I manage to open them enough to stumble into the bathroom. I stare at myself in the mirror and try to open my eyes wide, but they stay squinty and pink. I stick my tongue out at myself and shut off the light.

"Penny," Gram calls from downstairs, "you're going to be late."

I sigh and walk to my closet. I flip past a bunch of clothes that I haven't worn since I got here. In the City, I would dress to be noticed. Here I try to dress to disappear. I yank on a pair of cords peeking out from the top shelf in my closet, but they don't budge. I pull harder, and a whole stack of sweaters falls on top of my head. I pick up the sweater on top, a navy blue one with just the tiniest hole in the sleeve. To climb out of the closet I have to kick aside a suitcase that I haven't bothered to unpack.

"Penny," Gram calls again. *Coming,* I think. I quickly get dressed, staying in the T-shirt I slept in. I don't even bother with a hairbrush. I just pull my hair back into an elastic, flipping it over and over until it's a tiny mound at the base of my head. I search the room for my Chucks, even checking under the bed, until I remember that they're downstairs still in the washer. *Perfect.* I pull an old pair, with paint splatters all over them, out of my closet. I can pinpoint where each color came from. Green from when I painted my old bedroom. Pink from my mom's gallery. Blue and gray from the art project at the MoMA camp last summer. As I pull my shoes on I keep trying to come up with a way to get out of school, but I don't think Gram is going to fall for the whole *thermometer-on-the-lightbulb* trick.

From the bottom of the stairs, I can see Gram standing with her back to me, stirring something on the stove. I take a deep breath and prepare myself to give her the silent treatment. I know it's not her fault that my parents are separated. It's not her fault they're selling the apartment, but I feel like she's in on it and I'm tired of being outside of everything. I try not to talk, but as I walk across the living room and into the kitchen, I see someone else is sitting at the table.

"What are you doing here?" It comes out louder than I want it to.

Tally looks up from her bowl, tilts her head at me, and half smiles. Her hair is pulled back from her face with a headband that matches the tips of her hair, which are now hot pink instead of blue. I pull out one of the chairs farthest from Tally and sit down. She is still looking at me, her eyebrows raised. I brace myself for the question, *You okay?* But she just shakes her head slightly and takes a bite of her oatmeal. I know she's dying to say something, but maybe we haven't known each other long enough, or maybe she wants to wait until later when we're alone.

Gram walks over from the stove, the pot and a bowl in her hands. She stops and stares at me. "What happened to you?" she asks. "You look like something Oscar dragged in," she says, nodding toward my cat on the window seat.

"Thanks," I mumble. "Why aren't you at the bakery?" I ask, trying to change the subject. So much for giving her the silent treatment.

"Your mom said she could handle it, and I was feeling tired this morning, so I just decided to stay in bed a little longer." She puts the bowl down in front of me with a *thunk* and spoons some oatmeal into it. Then she sits down at the table. "Tally thought she'd come by and walk with you," Gram says. Tally nods and takes another bite of oatmeal. "If you hurry, you'll still have time to get changed before school."

Sorry, Tally mouths at me when Gram's not looking. I just roll my eyes.

"Fine." I push away from the table and start toward the stairs.

"Wait," Tally says. She reaches into her backpack and pulls out some green fabric. "Here," she says, balling it up and tossing it to me. I catch it and unfold it, realizing it's a T-shirt. My own drawing is staring up at me. I flip it over. RPS FOR THE ARK is written across the back in letters that look like they came from an old typewriter. I smile at the shirt and then at Tally.

"I'll be right back," I say. I hear Gram's voice when I'm about halfway up the stairs. I know she's talking loud enough so that I'll overhear.

"Maybe now she'll stop feeling so sorry for herself," she says.

I feel heat on my cheeks, but this time it's not because I'm embarrassed or sad, but because I'm mad. The problem is, I can't figure out whether I'm mad at Gram for saying it or mad at myself because she's right.

"Do you want to talk about it?" Tally asks, slowly plucking apart a cattail she picked when we crossed the bridge into town. Tiny fluffs of seed float up from her fingers as we walk. "Sometimes it helps," she says when I don't answer. I want to talk to her, but I don't know where to start. Do I tell her that my parents are communicating only through me and attorneys now? Do I tell her they're selling our apartment? Do I tell her my biggest fear, that it isn't going to be "fine"?

"Looks like it's going to rain," Tally says. I look up and see the heavy clouds pushing down on us.

"Perfect," I say.

Tally misses the tone of my voice or just chooses to ignore it. "I know, right?" she says with a smile. "The rain is going to keep everyone inside at lunch. We're going to make a killing."

"Tally, what are you talking about?"

"The T-shirts," she says. "*Your* T-shirts. They go on sale today." She pulls the last clump of seeds out of the cattail and tosses them into the air. The wind catches them, sending them up into the trees. She puts her hand on my arm and stops, making me stop, too. "Do you know how to do it?" she asks.

"Um, yeah," I say. "Selling T-shirts? I think I can manage that."

"No." She puts her hand out in a fist. "RPS." She quickly runs through the three options. "I can teach you." I squint at her, trying to figure out if she's serious. She just smiles at me. "Really," she says. "A lot of people just think it's luck."

"I think *most* people do," I say.

"Well, that's where *most* people are wrong," she says. "Here, hold your hand out." I make a fist and put it up near hers. "Okay," she says. "Remember, you throw on four." I keep watching her face. We're standing in the middle of the sidewalk in front of the school, and people have to squeeze around us, but Tally doesn't seem to notice. "Ready?" she asks. I nod. We pump our fists three times and then I leave mine closed. Tally has her hand flat, palm down. "Nice," she says. "Rock is an aggressive first throw." I look back up at her face, trying to predict when

she's going to start laughing. "Okay, let's see what else you got."
I put my fist out again; this time I form scissors. Tally has her
hand in a fist. She smiles and puts her hands in the pockets of
her hoodie. "I can teach you," she says. "It's not hard."

"I don't understand," I say. We start walking again. "I mean,
it's pretty simple, right? It's not like there's any strategy," I say.

"Okay, then," Tally says. "Then how did I just beat you
twice?"

"Um, luck?"

She sighs loudly. I follow her up the steps and into the side
door of the school. We stop at her locker, where she puts away
her backpack and gets out her books for first period. The can
of lard is still there, still perched on top of her books. She pushes
her locker shut with a click and turns toward me.

"I knew you were going to throw rock first. It's the easiest and
the most obvious move. It's also the safest move for a rookie."

I shrug. "Maybe," I say.

"Before the second round, I said: 'Let's see what else you
got.' So, of course you aren't going to throw rock again. The
next obvious throw is scissors."

"Why not paper?" I ask.

"Because I just threw paper. Scissors was the only move that
neither of us had used yet. Plus, paper is the hardest move. You
have to twist your wrist and throw at the same time."

"Why can't you just do this?" I ask, putting my hand out flat
with my thumb up.

"Vertical paper is a no-no in professional play."

I'm still trying to find the irony, trying to find the teasing in her eyes, but it's not there. "Okay, Tally," I say, smiling. "Will you teach me?"

"Of course," she says. The first bell rings, making me jump slightly. "We're going to be late," she says. "Meet me in front of the cafeteria at lunch." I nod and start walking toward my locker. "Wait," she says. "I almost forgot." Tally rummages in her backpack and pulls out two bars wrapped in cellophane. "Here." She hands them to me. "Lunch." I flip them over. "It's pemmican."

"It's what?" I ask.

"Trust me," Tally says, and then disappears into the crowd of kids pushing past. I sigh and look at the bars she gave me. Some sort of energy bars. From the label it looks like they might have been the *first* energy bars, way before PowerBars, but then again maybe they're just purposely retro. I stuff the bars into the front pocket of my hoodie. *Trust her.* I pull up on the latch of my locker.

The smell hits me as I open the door. There on top of my books is a plastic plate. I have to step back to catch my breath. It's one of my cupcakes—at least it used to be. The smell is coming from what's been stuck in the middle of it. Where there used to be an icing fish jumping on the end of a fisherman's line, now there's an actual fish. A small one, but it's been in there all night. I take out the plate and drop it into the trash can at the end of the hall. As I walk back to my locker to get out my now smelly books, I hear it behind me. I don't even bother to turn around to see who it is. It doesn't really matter who's laughing. Whether I have to convince my mom that we need to go back or I have to move into my dad's new place, in a few weeks I'll be gone and Hog's Hollow will just be a distant nightmare.

chapter eleven

$\mathcal{W}$hat do you think?" Tally is sitting on a folding chair behind a long table just outside the cafeteria. Stacks of RPS T-shirts teeter in front of her and Blake. Tally had the shirts made in three different colors: blue, orange, and olive.

"They're awesome," I say. "People have been coming up to me all morning and asking about my shirt."

"Did you tell them we'd be selling them at lunch?" she asks. I nod. I step to the side to make room for a group of girls. They finally pick shirts, all getting blue.

"Thank you for your business," Blake says, taking their money. He shoves the bills into a shoe box. There are several bars of pemmican, just like the ones Tally gave me, on the table in front of him. He takes a bite of one and makes a face, but he swallows it and smiles in Tally's direction.

Looking beyond them into the cafeteria, I can see that a bunch of kids have pulled the RPS T-shirts over their own shirts. Apparently Tally was right. A lot of people are into RPS.

Except for Charity's friends. One of the Lindseys walks by with Charlotte, very obviously ignoring the merchandise.

"I told you it would rain," Tally says. "Now everyone has to come inside for lunch."

"How did you get them to let you sell them here?" I ask.

Blake rolls his eyes. "She had photos of the animals at the ARK."

I raise my eyebrows at Tally.

"I did what I had to," she says with a smile. Then she picks up a bar of pemmican and takes a bite. She is only slightly more convincing about its taste appeal than Blake was. I start to ask again what's going on, but Tally turns her attention to a group of soccer players making a mess of a stack of extra-extra-large shirts.

"Hey." A familiar voice makes me turn. Marcus picks up one of the shirts and holds it up. He flips it over to look at the back.

"Penny designed them," Tally says, winking at me.

He looks over at me and smiles. "They're cool," he says.

"Oh, hi, Marcus." Charity pushes herself between us, actually elbowing me slightly to get me to back up. Her friends manage to create a human barrier between me and Marcus.

The way they move, it's like they are a pack of wolves, circling their prey. Charity looks at the shirt Marcus is holding as if it's covered in mold.

"Aren't these cool?" Marcus says.

She smiles and touches his arm. "That color looks good on you," she says, sidestepping his question.

Marcus hands two fives to Blake. Then he pulls the shirt over his head. Charity's right. The color does look good on him. He picks up his notebook and lunch. "See you around," he says, and I think he means everyone. Then, just before he walks into the cafeteria, he adds one word: "Penny."

Charity tries very hard not to react.

"Are you buying, or just looking?" Tally asks.

"Neither," Charity says.

Tally takes another bite of the bar in her hand and places it on the table so that the wrapper is faceup. I notice she positions it so that Charity can see the label. With the little puffin or whatever bird is right above the words ALL NATURAL. NO PRESERVATIVES. Charity looks at it for a long moment before Charlotte says, "What's RPS?"

"Ridiculous, Pathetic, Stupid," Charity says.

"Rock, Paper, Scissors," Tally says over her.

Charlotte looks at her for a moment. "As in the game?" Tally nods.

"See?" Charity says. "Stupid."

"The shirts *are* kind of cool . . ." Charlotte says tentatively.

Charity glares at her. "I guess, if you like *old* things," she says. She turns and smirks at me.

"Vintage," Tally says.

"Faux vintage," Blake says. This even makes Charlotte smile, but Charity still looks like she's been sucking on a lemon. A lemon Jolly Rancher maybe.

"Are you done looking at this stuff?" Charity asks. Charlotte puts the T-shirt down slowly, but even after she lets go, she keeps looking back at it. Charlotte and the three Lindseys follow Charity into the cafeteria.

"Okay, I know why she hates me, but what does she have against you guys?" I ask.

Blake shrugs. "She hates whimsy."

"Maybe she wanted a hundred percent cotton," Tally says.

"No, really," I say.

Tally sighs and looks past me. "Remember how Blake said I was banned from Hog's Hollow Days?" I nod and see Blake smirking. "Remember how I also said you weren't the only one dragged here against her will?" I nod again. "Well, let's just say I was pretty angry when I first moved here."

"Pretty angry?" Blake asks.

"Okay, I was really angry. I just got mad. Mad at my dad, at myself. I got mad at everything. I mean, at least until I just decided to make the best of it while I'm here."

Blake looks at his shoes and pushes his hands a little deeper into his front pockets. Something has pulled the smile from his face, and I wonder if it's just the thought of Tally leaving. And what she's saying is a little too close to what I know I should be doing. Suddenly I feel like the star of a bad public service announcement. This one is titled Just Deal with It.

Tally does her half smile and elbows Blake, who shakes himself, as if he was somewhere else and the elbow brought him back. "You tell her," she says.

Blake takes a breath. "Okay, you know how every female between the ages of twelve and eighteen in the tricounty area wants to be Hog Queen?"

"Not every," Tally says.

"Well, last year, the H.O.G.—"

"The Hog's Hollow Organizational Group," Tally says.

"Shouldn't that be the H.H.O.G.?" I ask.

"We are not really talking about higher-thinking people here," Tally says.

"Anyway," Blake says, "the H.O.G. decides to do away with the talent portion of the pageant. All of a sudden Tally, the new girl none of us knew, is everywhere, telling everyone that we are 'subjugating our young girls to a male-dominated paradigm.'" Blake turns to Tally. "Is that right?"

"Something like that," Tally says.

"Turns out that once they decided to take out the talent part, it became just a beauty contest, not a scholarship pageant. Anyway, she called all these feminist groups, and suddenly instead of a rehearsal, there was a protest."

"It wasn't just that I was looking to start a fight," Tally says. "I mean, I really do think beauty contests are degrading to women. No offense to your mom."

"I agree," I say. And the weird thing is, the mom I know would agree, too.

"Word got out that the reason the H.O.G. was trying to get rid of the talent portion was because of the chairman," Blake says.

"Chairperson," Tally says.

"Who was the chair*person*?" I ask.

"Mrs. Wharton." Blake grins. "Turns out Charity doesn't really have any talents."

I look into the cafeteria. Charity is sitting right next to Marcus, and I mean *right* next to him. Like if she sat any closer, she'd be sitting in his lap. She laughs at something he says and puts her hand on his arm. She leans toward him a bit, and I can feel my face heating up. It's then that she looks directly at me and smiles.

"She's pretty good at being mean," I say.

"She'd get crowned Hog Queen for sure if all she had to do was look pretty and be mean," Tally says. She pulls the rest of the pemmican bar out and stares at it for a moment, as if she's having an argument with it in her head. I guess the bar wins, because she puts it back down without taking a bite.

"So are you going to tell me?" I ask. I gesture toward the half-eaten bar on the table.

"I'll give you a hint: read the ingredients."

I pull one of the pemmican bars out of my pocket and read the wrapper. *Dried fruit, organic flour, lard.* What's with Tally and lard? I can't ask her, because now she's helping two guys in backward baseball caps find the right size shirt.

Most of me says to forget about all of this. By the time the festival comes around and Charity is up onstage vying for the crown, I'll have figured out a way to get my old life back. I'll be back in the City and telling all my friends about this and they'll be laughing and saying, "No way!" I'll have to keep saying "Way!" because they'll never believe a place like this exists. Unfortunately it's only most of me and not all. There's this tiny part of me that actually does care about all of this, and I need to get out of here before that part takes over.

I'm supposed to deliver the message about the apartment papers to my mom and I will, but only if she talks to me first. I know it's stupid. I know it's just a dumb game that I'm playing, but we've been in the house together, just the two of us, for almost three hours and she hasn't said one word to me. Not one. Since we've moved here, she keeps drifting further and further away, drifting back just enough to make a comment about how what I'm wearing or what I'm doing is wrong before she floats away again. If she isn't going to talk to me, then I'm not going to talk to her. I even put my shoes on the couch, but all she did was look at my feet and frown. She's been going through pictures, putting some in a box marked ME and some in a box marked PETER. I notice that all of the photos of their wedding go in my dad's box. I'm not an idiot. It's not like I need a big flashing neon sign to tell me that things have gotten worse between them since we moved to Hog's Hollow. But for once I'd like someone to just talk to me. I want to shout that at the back of my mother's head: *Just talk to me!* But I don't, because maybe if no one says anything out loud, it can still change.

Oscar walks through, holding his stuffed bear in his mouth, and my mother smiles over at him. The cat gets a smile. She doesn't even look at me when I stand up. I walk into the library and sit down in front of the computer. I check my e-mail. Nothing. I e-mailed my two best friends in the City last night, mostly questions about what they're doing, but also wanting to talk to someone about things. Normally I'd just call or text one of them, but it feels weird now. I feel the same disconnect that I have with my dad. Like everyone is pretending that everything is normal and nothing has changed, but the reality is that everything has changed and nothing feels normal at all.

The phone rings and my mother answers it. I brace myself, hoping it's not my father.

"It's Tally," my mom says. So, officially I should tell her about the papers because she talked to me, but she *had* to talk to me, so it doesn't count. I'm not sure what I'm trying to prove. I mean, the papers are going to get signed and they are going to sell the apartment and no one's going to tell me anything until it's done.

"Hello?" I say when I pick up the phone.

"What are you doing right now?" Tally asks.

I look around the room for a moment before admitting the obvious. "Nothing."

"Good," she says. "Then grab your umbrella and get down here. I have something to show you." The phone goes dead.

I'm not sure I'm up for being around other people right now. I think about calling her back. Think about making up some reason that I can't go, but then my mother walks past on her way to the stove and she doesn't even look in my direction.

"I'm going to Tally's," I say, my hand already on the back doorknob. She looks at me and nods, then considers the kettle in her hand. I pause for a moment with the door partly open. She looks so sad. I should say something. I want to say something, but I don't know what. I start to ask if she would rather I stay, if she wants to talk or play chess or make cookies, but then she looks at me again, the frown back on her face.

"Close the door. You're letting all the heat out."

I shake my head, grab my windbreaker off the back hook, and put it on, pulling the hood over my head. I have to run all the way down to Tally's to keep from getting drenched, but the cold feels good on my face. I let my hood fall away from my head and feel my hair whip behind. I wonder if Marcus feels like this when he runs. Like he's able to get a couple of steps ahead of everything.

I can see the lights from Tally's house up ahead. They seem to glow in the fog. I feel winded when I slow down in front of the stairs leading up to her house. As I climb the warped steps, I think about the problem with running from your trouble. The problem is in the stopping. The whole time you think you're getting away from everything, the trouble is running like mad, too, trying to catch up with you. And it doesn't slow down when you do—it keeps on sprinting. So when trouble finally reaches you, it hits you hard.

chapter twelve

*Y*ou have got to see this," Tally says, pulling the sleeve of my jacket and leading me to her computer. Almost the whole screen is filled with an image of a can of lard. Along the bottom are some of those before-and-after photos you see of women on infomercials. The first shows each woman in a too-small bathing suit, standing in bad lighting. The second shows them smiling, in full makeup, and pushed and pulled and tucked until they look fit. I push my damp hair out of my eyes and sit in the other chair in front of the screen. I think about Tally's weird new eating habits.

"Tally, are you on a diet?" I ask. She pretends not to hear me and clicks the mouse. Another site pops up, this one much busier, with links for instruction manuals, videos, application forms, and something called "Domination." Tally clicks the *Play* button on one of the videos. First it's just a close-up of two pairs of hands in fists, then they do the triple up-and-down move. One hand opens into paper while the other forms scissors. "This is from last year's championship in Seattle." A girl who looks to be about our age is handed a trophy with three faux-bronze hands, one in each position. A guy behind her, wearing a Jedi costume, looks like he's about to cry.

"What's with Luke Skywalker?" I ask, pointing to him.

"There are all kinds of kooks who go to these things." I can't help but wonder what kind of kooks *we* are.

We watch the rest of the video as they run highlights from the competition. They actually have a reporter doing the voiceover, like it's a real sport. Tally clicks through more videos and I half watch, half listen as she talks about more strategies and tricks. She clicks the window closed, and there's the diet site again.

Beneath all the noise coming from the videos, I can hear music playing. Soft guitar, slow and sad.

"What is that?" I ask.

Tally squints at the screen. "Just a Web site I'm fooling around with."

"No, I mean the music."

"Just music," she says, quickly muting it.

"I liked it," I say, but she's already up and on her way to the kitchen. She takes out two glasses and opens the refrigerator. She stands there, staring at the carton of milk, the pitcher of lemonade.

"Do you ever talk to your dad?" Tally asks, still peering into the refrigerator.

"Yeah," I say, although the truth is I don't very much. "He's pretty busy, though." He's always been busy, and not just since we moved here. Too busy for me at least.

Tally grabs the lemonade and shoves the refrigerator shut with her hip. She hits the door too hard, sending several magnets spinning across the floor. I slide my foot out of my sneaker and use my toes to pick up a broccoli magnet. She watches me and smiles. "That's a real talent you have there."

She pours me a glass of lemonade and slides it toward me. "My dad's busy, too," she says. She looks at me, as if daring me to say something.

"Where is he right now?" I ask.

She takes a long drink from her glass, watching me over the rim. When she doesn't answer right away, I wonder if maybe I've overstepped. I'm about to tell her never mind, that it's none of my business, but she finally answers. "Don't know." She pulls a sheet of paper off the refrigerator and reads it. "Looks like Seattle." She tosses the paper on the counter. "Maybe."

"Why maybe?" I ask.

"Probably," she says. She finishes her lemonade and puts her glass back on the counter. Hard. *Probably* sounds only slightly more solid than *maybe*.

"Do you miss him?" I ask.

She shrugs and picks up her father's schedule. She folds it in half, then half again. She flips it as she folds, making hard creases with the side of her fingernail. "Sure," Tally says. "Of course I miss him." She keeps fiddling with the schedule, folding and refolding, not looking at me. "It was really good for a while, you know?" Her voice gets so quiet I have to lean forward to hear her. "It was just him and me. I'd always sit right up front when he played." She smiles at the folded paper in her hands. "At first it was just small places, clubs and bars, but then one of his songs started getting a lot of play time." She peeks at me through her hair. I nod, encouraging her. Her face is so sad, I feel like hugging her, but she's still messing with the paper. Tally looks down again and continues. "He got better gigs. Bigger venues. He started leaving me back at the hotel sometimes." She smiles over at me. "I used to raid the vending machines and stay up watching television or playing on his laptop until he got back."

"That sounds fun," I say. She nods. "And lonely."

Tally frowns. "Yeah, sometimes." Her voice gets softer. "A couple of times he didn't come back until the next day."

From the look on her face I'd be willing to bet that it was more than a couple of times.

"Were you scared, all alone like that?" I ask.

"He said he didn't have a choice." She looks up at me. I nod, unconvinced. "It wasn't like I could just tag along all the time, you know?"

"Then what happened?" I ask gently. "What brought you here?"

Her eyes get wet, and she brushes them with the back of her hand. "There was this one time he didn't come back for three days."

I can't keep the shock from my face.

"The maids were coming by the room, wanting to clean it. And someone from the front desk kept calling and asking when we were checking out. I didn't know what to tell them. I mean, I wasn't supposed to let anyone in. Or go anywhere." A couple of tears splash onto the counter.

"What did you do?" I ask, trying to think of what I'd do if I was stranded in a hotel somewhere.

"I called Poppy. When I told her where I was, she got on a plane." She wipes her eyes with the sleeve of her sweater. "Just because I said I needed her." From the tone of her voice, Tally still seems awed by what Poppy did for her, as if she didn't deserve it.

"You did the right thing," I say.

She nods halfheartedly. "It didn't exactly win Poppy any points with my dad. That was over a year ago."

I don't know what to say. When we first met, she told me she was just here for a while. That her dad was coming back to get her soon.

She opens up the paper, revealing a sleek airplane, all points and angles. She lifts the plane and looks down its back. She pulls back her arm and lets the plane fly. It goes straight and fast, the way my paper airplanes never do. Until the end, when, instead of landing smoothly, it suddenly just drops to the floor, its folds opened up.

The phone rings, making both of us jump. Tally wipes her eyes again and sniffs before picking it up. "Talk to me," she says. She listens. I take a sip of lemonade and try to let her story sink in. "Hey, Monkey Toes," Tally says, her voice happy. I look up and see she's smiling at me. "Want to go somewhere?"

"Where to?" I ask.

"It's a surprise," Tally says, making her eyes go big. "You in?"

"Sure," I say. I drain the last of my lemonade and put my glass in the sink. I follow Tally onto the front porch and out onto the road. I want to say something hopeful, something that will make everything better, but I can't even make my own life okay. How can I possibly make Tally's life okay?

But she seems back to her old silly self. "Monkey Toes," Tally says, pulling her hair back into an elastic. "I like it. It could totally be your RPS name."

"I have to be Monkey Toes?"

"It could be worse," she says, checking Poppy's mailbox among the clump of them at the entrance to the cove.

"Monkey Face?" I ask.

"Yeah, that would be worse." Tally flips through several envelopes, then puts them all back in the box. "But I meant Blake's." We head out onto the main road, where she stops. "Blake's mom is picking us up," Tally says. We wait, watching the storm clouds blow across the sky. "You'll like her. Although, sometimes she's too mom-ish," Tally says, stuffing her hands in her pockets. "Always worrying if I'm warm enough or if I've had enough to eat."

"My mom does that, too," I say. *Or did,* I think.

"Between Poppy and Blake's mom, I've got a double helping."

I want to ask about her real mom, but I figure talking about one missing parent was enough for today. So instead I ask about Blake. "What's the deal with Blake's hair?"

Tally laughs. "When I first moved here he had this sad mullet thing." I squinch up my face, making Tally laugh harder. "It was bad." She shakes her head. "He was my first friend when I moved here. My only friend." She's quiet for a moment, thinking. Then she smiles at me. "So, want to know Blake's nickname?" She doesn't wait for me to answer. "Major Manure."

I raise my eyebrows. "That *is* worse," I say. "Why?"

"One, he lost a bet. And two—you'll see." Tally lifts her hand to wave as a red farm truck slows down and pulls onto the shoulder. As we walk toward the truck, a rich earthy smell gets stronger and stronger. Tally pulls open the passenger door and slides into the middle. I say "hi" when she introduces me to Blake's mom. It isn't until we're under way that I realize what's in the back. Even a city girl like me knows what manure looks like, and lucky me, now I'm aware of what it smells like when a mountain of it is about three inches away. Tally laughs when she sees my face.

"Sorry about the smell," Blake's mom says.

"What smell?" I ask, making them both laugh. I laugh, too, but the whole way to their house, I breathe through my mouth.

The air in the greenhouse is thick, so thick you can see it moving in the breeze from the overhead fans. "It's a little humid in here," I say. Blake just nods, but I notice that the points of his hair look like they're wilting a bit. Tally is near the back of the greenhouse, trying to open one of the crank windows. Blake walks past with some sort of brown liquid in a bucket. He ladles a spoonful over each plant as he passes.

"Yum, huh?" Tally says, walking back over to me. "Poop Soup." I wrinkle my nose and she laughs. "It's all-natural." She laughs again as my face stays contorted.

Blake walks past again and I catch another whiff of the mixture. *"Manure du jour,"* he says. He makes his way down a long line of tomato plants.

"Cream of Crap," Tally says.

"Dung Drop Surprise," Blake says. By now they are both laughing. I can't help but smile.

"Jus d'excrément," Tally says.

"Lame," Blake says. He walks back over to us and points the spoon at me. "Now you."

I close my eyes and try to run through all the words I know for poo. "Reese's Feces?"

Blake squints at me for a moment. "Not bad," he says. "For a beginner." He puts the bucket down beneath the table and pulls out cardboard trays. He thrusts one into my hands and gives one to Tally, who tries to protest. "Oh, hush. It's not like you have anything better to do." She frowns at him and he frowns back, making her smile. "Here, Penny, you take the middle aisle." Tally makes her way over to the right. "Only pick the red ones," Blake says loudly. She waves the back of her hand at him and disappears behind a forest of tomato plants.

"Couple weeks ago Tally was here helping me and she picked a bunch of unripe ones. My mom had a fit. Luckily she convinced her buyer that green tomatoes were all the rage." He reaches into the leaves of a plant. When he pulls his hand out he's clutching an orange-and-red-striped tomato about the size of a grapefruit. "Okay, this is what you're looking for," he says. He pushes his thumb gently against the tomato and pulls it away, leaving a faint mark. "Pretty, aren't they?" I nod. "They have a gruesome name, though. Bloody Butcher." He puts the tomato in my box. He works alongside me, trying to look like he's not checking every tomato I pick.

"So what's the mystery with Mr. Fish?" I ask, trying to keep my voice neutral. What I really want to know is more about Marcus, but talking to Blake about him is too weird.

Blake pulls a tomato off the next plant and examines it. It's dark purple, almost black. "He's building something up in the woods above town," he says.

"Building what?" I ask.

"Not sure," Blake says. "Radio towers or something." He puts another tomato in my box. "Maybe he's trying to contact aliens."

I keep picking, working up my courage for another question. Finally I ask, "Do you know Marcus very well?"

"I did," Blake says. "I mean, before." He's quiet for a minute. All I can hear is the whir of the fans above us. "I don't think anyone knows him now," he says.

"Except Charity," I say.

"I doubt it," he says. He makes his way around the corner to the next row, and I think we're finished, but he pauses. "Don't let Charity get to you. She's mostly harmless."

Mostly, I say to myself as he walks away, his box slapping against his leg. I'm not so sure. I've seen her be nasty to other kids, but with me she turns the meanness volume way up. She doesn't even try to lower her voice when she's ragging on me. About my hair, or how I'm dressed, or just how I talk. And she never lets up. But it's the Marcus stuff that drives me really bananas. She's always talking to him or walking with him. And she makes sure I notice.

"Hey!" Tally yells over the buzz of the fans. "When do we get a break?"

"When you've actually done some work!" Blake yells back, making me laugh. Not even the thought of Charity can ruin my mood for long. I vow never to eat another tomato as I fill my box. Every once in a while Tally yells a gripe about working conditions or child labor laws, and Blake tells her to hush and get back to work. The humidity is making my hair stick to my neck, but as I get into a rhythm of picking, I realize I'm humming—something I haven't done in a long time.

After working in the hot greenhouse for more than an hour, I'm happy to take a break. We sit on the back porch of Blake's house. Me in an Adirondack chair overlooking the pond, Blake and Tally squished on the glider.

"So how come you don't have seventeen pets?" I ask Blake. Tally has been going on and on about this new kitten at the ARK. I'm just not sure my cat, Oscar, is ready for a sibling.

"Allergies," Blake says. "I have to take an antihistamine to get within a hundred feet of Tal's house." He kicks the ground and the glider starts to move. "Of course I'm allergic to everything. Animals, peanuts . . . you name it." As if on cue, he sneezes. He smiles at me. "Living in the country is rough when you have allergies." He takes a handkerchief out of his pocket—one of those blue ones you always see on cowboys—and blows his nose. "What was it like living in Manhattan?"

"I don't know," I say. "I guess it was like living anywhere else." Blake takes a bite of his tomato, eating it like an apple. He swears it's good.

"Yeah, except there's actually things to do there," Tally says. She pulls her knees up, hooking her heels on the edge of the glider. "There we could be going to museums and bookstores and sitting around in cafés." She sounds wistful, and it makes me miss the City for a moment. "Here, we have what? Picking tomatoes." Tally leans into Blake with her shoulder. "No offense." Blake smiles at her with tomato in his mouth, making Tally wrinkle her nose.

"Do you miss it?" Blake asks me.

I nod and look at Tally, but she's rubbing at the toe of her sneaker, trying to make a tomato stain go away. "Some things," I say.

"Your friends?" Tally asks. She doesn't look up when she talks—just keeps rubbing the toe of her sneaker.

I haven't been in contact with anyone that much. I want to be, but I'm afraid that if I tell my old friends about my new friends, they might make fun of them. They wouldn't understand it if I told them I picked tomatoes and had fun doing it. "It's mostly my dad I miss." I feel like a jerk as soon as the words are out of my mouth. After what Tally told me, I have no right to whine.

Before I can think of something to say to make it better, Tally looks up at me. "It's hard," she says sympathetically, and I just nod.

"Know what else is hard?" Blake asks. We both look at him. "Listening to you two sometimes."

"What do you mean?" Tally asks.

"Girls are so dumb." Tally squints at him threateningly, but he continues. "With guys it's simple. When I hang out with my friends, we just chill. You two are all with the *'Oh, I wonder if so-and-so likes me.'* " Blake makes his voice high when he says it.

"Is that supposed to be me?" Tally asks.

"Yes, you." Then he points at me. "And Penny. All of your kind."

"Are you as offended as I am?" she asks me, pretending to be insulted. I nod.

"I'm going to end this thing," Blake says. "Tally, do you take Penny to be your friend?"

She looks at me and says, "I do."

"Penny, do you take Tally to be your friend?"

"I do, too." A tiny spark glows inside of me, one that I didn't even know had gone out.

"I now pronounce you two friends," Blake says. He kicks the ground to make their glider swing. "Now can we please talk about something more interesting?"

"What could possibly be more interesting than our friendship ceremony?" Tally asks.

"Anything," he says. "As long as we don't have to talk about how we *feel* about it." Blake takes another bite of tomato and then throws the stem end over the fence to the chickens. We laugh as one of them grabs it and runs off, making the others chase it around the yard. If only my City friends could see me now.

chapter thirteen

Sunday morning Gram gets me up early to pick blueberries. I mean early—like dark-thirty. She wants to make enough jam to last the winter. Even though it's before dawn, Mom is already gone. She's been working long hours at the bakery. Twice this week I found her asleep on the couch, a book tented on her chest and her reading glasses still perched on her face. I've tried to help, but Mom and Gram keep reminding me that school comes first.

"I can see my breath," I say, dropping a handful of berries into my pail. Gram just smiles at me—or I think she does by the look in her eyes. Her mouth is mostly covered by her scarf.

"Autumn is just around the corner," Gram says. She rakes her fingers through the bush, making blueberries fall into her pail. "You'll love the fall here, Penny. Once the leaves start turning, the hills look like they're on fire."

She's quiet for a moment, then she looks over at me,

sliding her scarf down so I can see her whole face. "How are you doing?"

"I'm cold," I say.

"I meant more in general."

If it were Tally I'd say I was generally cold, but I know better than to push my luck with Gram. "I'm okay, I guess."

"You want to try again?" Gram asks. She rakes more blueberries into her pail. Already she's more than doubled my haul.

I sigh. "It's hard." I pull another berry from the bush I'm working on and pop it into my mouth, buying myself a little thinking time.

"You already have a couple of friends," Gram says.

I nod. *And enemies,* I think. "I like being with you. And I like school—mostly."

"Any cute boys there?"

"Gram! I am not having *that* conversation with you." She laughs, and I immediately give in. "Well, there is one. . . ."

"Mmm-hmm. One is all you need."

Yeah, too bad there are at least two of us interested in him, I think.

We work for a while longer. Just as the sky is starting to brighten, Gram tells me she has enough berries for two cases. She's nice enough not to mention that she has about seven times as many berries in her pail as I do in mine. We start walking back down the hill toward her house. The closer we get, the more we can smell the ocean. Gram stops when we hit the sand

and looks out over the water. I think she's going to make some comment about the gulls or the clouds or some other part of nature she's forever trying to make me notice, but she doesn't.

"Your parents love you," she says.

"I know." Coming from Gram, it doesn't sound hollow. "I just wish—" *Wish what? I don't know anymore.* "I just wish she'd talk to me," I say.

"You should tell her that. Goodness knows I've tried."

I want to tell Gram that I've actually heard her trying. And I know Mom's just trying to shield me. Dad, too. But part of protecting someone is letting them know what they're being protected from.

"Just give it a little time," Gram says. I nod. Since it looks like we're staying for the near future and then some, I have time to give. A lot of time.

Monday, Gram leaves me a note, telling me she's out picking berries again. She also leaves me fresh blueberry muffins for breakfast. Art has become my favorite class, and that's saying a lot, since it's the only class I have with Charity. Miss Beans steps to the center of the room. "This weekend, I'd like all of you to start thinking about what your contribution to the parade is going to be." She passes around old HHHS yearbooks, featuring photos of parade floats. The floats look just like you would expect. There's a truck hauling the biggest pumpkin I've ever seen. The Boy Scouts have a float about first aid. They must have been practicing some pretty advanced stuff. A couple of the kids have realistic-looking head wounds, and three of them seem to be missing limbs. Tally and I point out the funny ones to each other before passing the yearbooks to the next table.

"Remember, if your float idea is selected," Miss Beans says, "you'll get to see your vision realized. Your float will carry the Hog Queen and her court."

"Awesome," Tally whispers. "I can hardly wait."

I try to picture my mother getting excited about riding around town on a farm trailer decorated with Styrofoam and crepe paper. The back table starts whispering and giggling. Tally makes another face at me and does a fake beauty queen wave, making me laugh. I look over at Charity and see her staring at me. She mouths something, but I can't decipher it. I know it's mean, though. It's obvious from her expression and the way everyone at her table has to cover their mouths to keep from laughing. She does her ice queen smile and looks away.

We keep passing yearbooks around as we start sketching our ideas. I'm just blocking in the trailer when I see Tally stop on a yearbook page and then slam the book shut. She quickly puts it in her lap.

"What is it?" I whisper. She just shakes her head. I look up and see Charity smiling at me again. "Show me." Tally shakes her head again and then shoves the book under her chair.

When it's time to clean up, I hang back while everyone else stacks their sketchbooks in their cubbies. I slide the yearbook out from under Tally's chair and open it in my lap. One of the pages is dog-eared, and on it I see an old photo of what must have been my mom. It's impossible to tell for sure, because the face has been drawn over with black ink. You know, the usual— glasses, mustache, black teeth. Underneath the photo someone crossed out her name and wrote in *Hog's Hollow Ho*.

My stomach twists. I rip the page out of the book and crumple the paper in my lap. I don't bother to hide it from Tally when she sits down.

"Aren't they clever?" Tally says loudly. "How do they think up these things? It must take them weeks." Then, under her breath, she says to me, "Don't let those morons get to you."

Miss Beans has been collecting the yearbooks from each table. When she comes over to us, I hand her ours and say in a wobbly voice, "This one has a page missing."

Before I can say any more, she looks into my eyes and says, "Hmm. I guess I need to be more careful about who I trust with these. Not everyone is as mature as you are, I'm afraid. Thanks for letting me know, Penny." She gives me a little pat on the shoulder before she walks away.

"She's totally onto them," Tally says.

"She'd have to be blind not to be," I say, wondering why Miss Beans doesn't do more to stop Charity. But I can feel some of the tension seeping out of me.

Tally elbows me and points out into the hall. Blake is leaning against the lockers, wearing his sunglasses and looking half asleep. His hair is hanging in his face, making him look less like a pineapple and more like a puppy. The bell rings, and he jumps.

"Late night?" Tally asks, ruffling his hair.

Blake smiles and nods, pushing away from the lockers. "The heater broke in one of the greenhouses. I was up most of the night hanging blankets across the windows to keep the plants from freezing." He yawns and leans against the wall while I get my lunch from my locker.

"Come on, sleepy," Tally says, pulling the sleeve of his jacket. After the frigid night, it's an oddly warm day. Way too warm for this time of year. We head out onto the front lawn, where Blake stretches out under a tree and promptly falls asleep.

"Are you going to submit a design for the parade?" Tally asks. I shrug and bite into my sandwich. "You should, Penny. I'll bet it'd win."

I chew, not sure what to say. Having my design built would be cool, but it's like every time I sort of get into a groove here, Charity is right there to push me off track again. I look over to the wall where a lot of people are sitting eating lunch. Charity is standing with some guy, laughing as she touches his arm. They're both looking at a book he's holding. Then I realize it's not some guy, but Marcus.

Tally is talking about the parade, about how much money we've raised for the ARK, about the movie she and Blake are going to see. I force myself to listen and not look back at the wall, back at Marcus. It's as if he's two people. One I like a lot. But the other one, the one who is always letting Charity hang off him, I'm starting to like a lot less. My sandwich is hard to swallow. I'm just so tired of everything. Tired of just taking it. I try to think what I'd do if this were happening at my school in the City. But maybe it's like I'm two people now, too—a "before" and an "after." I drop my sandwich onto my lunch bag. By the way it bursts apart, it's really more of a throw.

"Tell me about Charity," I say. Tally raises her eyebrows at me. "What's the saying? Know your enemy?"

"Know thine enemy," Blake mumbles. Then he yawns again and puts his arm over his eyes.

"Sleeping Beauty probably knows a lot more about her than I do," Tally says, smiling over at Blake. "My interactions with her have been limited to the pageant brouhaha last year and the fruitcake thing at the Winter Carnival." I want to ask *What fruitcake thing?,* but she keeps talking. "She was in France all last spring, doing some student exchange thing." She shrugs and reaches into her lunch sack. "I wish I knew more. It would make getting back at her easier." She pulls out her sandwich and lays it in front of her on the flattened bag. "All I really know is she's vain and mean and superficial."

"And dumb," Blake says from beneath his arm.

"And dumb," Tally echoes.

"And into Marcus," I say softly, glancing over to where they are still looking at the book spread on his lap.

Tally picks up her sandwich and then puts it back on the bag without taking a bite. "He's not into her," she says.

"You should tell him that," I say.

Blake just moans under his arm, earning a shove from Tally.

"If you don't like what we're talking about, stop eavesdropping," she says.

"What kind of sandwich is that? Cheese?" I ask, looking at the pieces of white goo peeking out from between her bread. Tally shakes her head and leans back on her hands. A group of Charity's friends walks by, and I notice them all looking at us. It's not so much us they're staring at, but Tally's sandwich. Tally has repeated the *spoon-in-the-can* trick several times, earning her weird eating habits a reputation. "When are you going to tell me what's going on?" I ask.

"I'll tell you what my sandwich is made out of," she says. She doesn't have to. I've already guessed: lard. I just shake my head. She opens her Ziploc full of grapes and pops one into her mouth. "What is lard?" she asks.

"Animal fat," I say. I look down at my sandwich. This whole conversation is taking away my appetite.

"More specific," Tally says. She watches me with a half smirk on her face. I shrug. I'm not much of an expert on lard. "Pig fat," she says. She pops two more grapes into her mouth and starts pushing everything back into her sack. She is careful to fold her sandwich so anyone watching would think she ate most of it. People start packing it in and walking toward the school. I shove the rest of my lunch into my sack and slip my sneakers back on.

Tally is still talking as she stands up and brushes off the back of her jeans. "Lard is the traditional source of fat in our diet. It wasn't until we started eating so many fat-free and low-fat foods that we all got fat." I nod, still wondering why the sudden interest in rendered pig fat. She's talking louder than she needs to, and I notice Charlotte listening off to one side. The first bell rings, clearing the lawn. I stand up. Blake seems to actually be asleep. Tally bends to try and wake him up. Charity and her friends are clustered at the door, watching us. Something's brewing. There are popping noises all around us.

"Oh man!" Tally says. She shakes Blake's shoulder. "Go!" she yells to me. "Hurry!" Blake sits up and rubs his eyes behind his sunglasses. I stand there, not sure what the noise is. The water is cold when it hits me. The sprinklers. Blake stands up on wobbling legs. All three of us run for the sidewalk, but it's a long way, and by the time we get there, we're drenched.

"Talk about a rude awakening," Blake says, shaking his head, sending droplets of water flying in all directions.

Tally peels off her sweatshirt and uses it to rub at her hair. "Since when do they water the lawn during the day?"

"Since Charity paid off the janitor," I say, wringing out my ponytail.

You-Know-Who and her friends are still on the front steps, now pointing and laughing at us, along with dozens of other people who have gathered there. Still more are watching from the windows overlooking the lawn.

"Everyone's looking," I say.

Tally turns toward the building and waves, making a few people laugh. Blake bows deeply, and the laughing gets louder. They both turn and look at me. I curtsy, holding out a fake skirt in my hands. Charity and her friends push through the crowd and walk back inside, but not before I see her face. She's no longer smiling.

"It's all in the way you spin things," Tally says as we walk inside. I now know that's Classic Tally. Spinning things. Blake holds out his arm and Tally takes it. By the time we enter the hallway, I'm smiling. Blake keeps doffing an invisible hat at everyone we pass, and Tally gives everyone her best queen wave.

Maybe she's right. Maybe I just need to spin things a little on my own instead of letting everything else spin me. I, too, wave at everyone hanging out of their classrooms to gawk at the three of us. I make sure to take a little extra time in front of Charity's classroom, giving her my best red carpet smile.

chapter fourteen

I can't believe I have been reduced to this. Sifting through garbage. Although to be honest, bakery garbage is probably pretty low on the disgust-o-meter. I mean, a butcher shop would be worse. I volunteered to close up partly just to have something to do. Tally and Blake are at the movies in Lancaster. Picking tomatoes with them is one thing. Going with them on, as they call it, "a nondate" is another. A movie on a Friday night? That's a date. The other reason I decided to stay late is because I am tired of always being the last to know everything. After my mom gave Gram another one of her *I'll talk to you later* looks, I decided I wasn't going to wait. I push past carrot peelings and dozens of strawberry tops. The envelope I'm looking for is blue. I saw my mother throw it away before she left. The fact that my mother, the Queen of Recycling, threw something in the trash was the big clue she was hiding it. I dig farther into the garbage, feeling old coffee grounds work their way up under my fingernails. Gram and Mom had this hushed discussion out on the back porch, and when they came back inside, they kept giving each other these looks across the kitchen. The longer we're here, the more my mom has been treating me like I'm four. She actually spelled something to Gram the other day, like I couldn't manage to figure that one out.

I keep digging, tipping the big trash can slightly so I can reach deeper. I push past eggshells and wads of plastic wrap. Finally I see it, way down at the bottom, resting on a pile of lemon rinds. I pull it out, scraping a blob of buttercream off the top. I open the envelope. Empty. I start to tip the can back up to standing, but another scrap of paper catches my eye. Unfortunately, that's all it is, a scrap, but the scrap has words on it, and among them are *separation agreement* and *assets* and *visitation*. I tip the can farther and look for the other pieces of the torn-up letter. I have to dump almost all of the garbage onto the floor, but I finally find them all. I sit on the rubber mat in front of the sink and piece them together. It's a cover letter from someone named Thomas J. Hall, Esq. It's written to my mother, but it says my father has a copy, too. You always think you're going to feel at least a little better when you find out the truth. I start scooping the trash back into the can, shoving the pieces of the letter in along with all the scraps and empty cartons. I think about saving it, but I'm not sure what I'd do with it. It's not like I'm going to keep it in my scrapbook at home.

Look, kids, this is when Mommy took a trip to Disney World, and here's when we visited the World's Biggest Ball of String. Oh, the coffee stains? That's a funny story. I had to dig it out of the trash. Yep, that's when I found out my mom and dad weren't just taking a break. That's when I found out that things were a lot worse than I thought.

It's dark by the time I lock the back door of the bakery behind me. I tried to call my dad, tried to make someone talk to me, but all I got was his voice mail. Some electronic voice telling me to leave a message or push five if I wanted to page him. I left a *Call me, I need to talk to you* message.

I start heading down Main Street. It's only a little after seven, but the whole town looks deserted. Add a few tumbleweeds and a hitching post or two and you'd have the perfect set for an Old West ghost town. The moon is just coming up over the trees. It's full and yellow, so round it looks like it could just roll across the sky. A harvest moon, my dad once taught me. I remember walking through Central Park with him when I was little, playing hide-and-seek with the moon as it appeared and disappeared among the skyscrapers. It's like the moon is the only thing connecting then to now.

I turn down the road to the beach, leaving asphalt for packed dirt and rock. I keep tripping on the rocks, because I'm watching the moon instead of my feet. I hear footsteps coming toward me, and I move to the side of the road to give whoever it is room.

I can see the silhouette of someone running. Before my brain can even process it, my heart starts beating faster. *Marcus.* I tuck my hair behind my ear, a nervous habit I wasn't aware of until Tally pointed it out. Of course now I notice it all the time. *Thank you, Tally.* If I had to come up with a list of things I wouldn't want Marcus to see me covered in, trash is pretty high up there. I tried to wash it off in the sink before I left, but I was in a hurry to get out of there, and I figured I'd just shower when I got home. So far he's seen me covered in paint, sand, tears, and now garbage.

"Hi," he says, when he spots me. I'm at a disadvantage (besides being covered in old coffee grounds and bits of eggshell). With the moon behind him, it's hard to see his face.

"Hi," I say. I try to think of something else, something funny maybe? Something smart about the moon. If I were talking to Tally, I'd have ten things to say, but all I can come up with is "hi," and I've already said that.

Marcus runs his hand over his hair. "I was hoping I'd see you," he says. Even though he just ran up the steep hill from the sand, he isn't even out of breath.

Wait. Did he just say he was hoping to see me? I do the hair tuck thing again, unsure of what to say. I want to ask why he talks to Charity at school and me only when no one's around. I want to ask him what makes him think I want to see him? Then it hits me. "Your sweatshirt. I keep meaning to get it back to you. I just wanted to wash it first." I know I'm talking too fast, my words coming out like they're tacked together. Even in the dark, I can see Marcus starting to smile. This only makes me talk faster. "I should have brought it up to school. I just . . ." I stop. What can I possibly say I was doing? Crying? Pulling dead fish out of my locker? Trash can diving?

"Penny," Marcus says. I exhale softly, realizing I've been holding my breath. "I wasn't thinking about my sweatshirt." I feel my cheeks heating up. I hear more footsteps coming up the road, but this time there's also the distinctive click of toenails on the rocks. "Brace yourself," Marcus says. Sam runs past him and slams into my legs. This time I'm ready for him. He's panting hard and trying to lick my fingers and do his chuffing thing, all at the same time. I laugh as Sam keeps licking me. "He can smell the bakery on you." I feel my cheeks heating up again. I probably smell like sour milk and banana peels. "Even in school, I can smell the vanilla and sugar when you walk by."

I look over at Marcus. It's his turn to blush. He combs his fingers through his hair. I wonder if Tally would tell him about *his* nervous habit. I want to believe that this Marcus, the one that's maybe flirting with me, is the real one. That the other one is just the school Marcus. But I'm me no matter where I am. I have enough half people in my life right now, I don't need any more.

"I guess I should head home," I say. Sam chuffs again and starts to head back down the hill toward the beach. Then he runs back toward us. He pushes his muzzle into my hands again, then turns and heads back down the hill.

"I think he wants us to follow him," Marcus says. "Can you walk for a few minutes?" Sam chuffs again, making both of us laugh.

"It's hard to say no to that." We start down the hill, walking close enough that I can feel the heat coming off Marcus's arm. I notice that the moon has climbed halfway up the sky. It's smaller now, regular moon size, and it makes me a little sad to think it moved so far away while I wasn't paying attention.

"See that ring around the moon?" Marcus says, surprising me that he, too, is looking at the moon. "That means there's a storm on the way. I learned all kinds of astronomy stuff as a kid," he explains, almost apologetically.

"I used to have those glow-in-the-dark stars and planets stuck to my ceiling at home," I say.

"Me, too," Marcus says, his voice happy. We start walking away from the lights glowing in Gram's house. I wonder if Mom and Gram are worried. Then I decide I don't care. If they aren't going to tell me things, I won't bother either.

"I used to live here," Marcus says when we draw even with his darkened house. Sam is already sitting on the bottom step leading to the porch, making me think he's probably been here with Marcus before. I look over at the Marcus, at the way wind is blowing his hair away from his forehead. "But then you probably already know that," he says.

I nod, making him laugh softly. "Small town."

He walks over to the steps leading up to the porch. "Here,"

he says, taking my hand. "Watch the third step. It's rotted through." We sit on the top step, watching the water. Sam hops over the broken step and sits in front of me, his tail making soft brushing sounds against the wood. He puts his head in my lap, leaning his weight against me. The wind whips through the dunes, pushing at us. Despite Sam's warmth on my lap, I shiver. "Cold?" Marcus asks. I shrug, but end up shivering again. "I can walk you home," he says. I shake my head. No amount of weather is going to move me from this step. Marcus slides closer until I can feel his leg against mine. He puts his hand behind me on the steps and leans toward me, so he almost, but not quite, has his arm around me. "Better?" he asks. I can feel his warm breath on the side of my neck. I just nod, feeling my face flush. We sit like that for so long that Sam starts snoring softly against my leg.

"Did you know that there are more than ten billion stars in the Milky Way alone?" Sam shifts against my leg and sighs deeply. "But that even on a really good night, with a new moon and no clouds, you can only see a couple thousand of them?" He leans toward me again, but this time it's to lift his hand toward the sky. "There's the Pleiades, and Ursa Major and Ursa Minor." He goes on to list some of the other constellations hovering over us.

"It's beautiful out here," I say. "One time my family spent a week on a lake in Maine. My dad took me out in the canoe one night. It was really cold. I didn't want to go at first, but once we got out on the water, it was amazing." I pause, suddenly shy, but I can feel Marcus beside me, listening. "The whole sky was filled—thousands of stars. We could even see the cleft in the Milky Way," I say.

"Not many people get to see that," he says. He chuckles softly. "Not many people even know what that is." Then he's quiet again, thinking. "Listen," Marcus says finally. And I do, but before he can say anything more, Sam lets out a snort that makes us both laugh. Marcus turns toward me, then looks back out over the water. "At the end of Hog Days . . ." He pauses again, making me smile. "I know, it's lame. I guess really lame, considering where you moved from." He's quiet again.

"The City wasn't that great," I say, and I mean it.

"Well then," Marcus says, and he leans forward a bit so that I can only see the side of his face. "There's this dance. . . ." He pauses for a moment and I hold my breath. "I wonder if you might like to go."

"I'd like that," I say. A tiny part of me wonders why he's not asking Charity, but I'm not about to ask *him* that.

He smiles at me—a real smile. "I'll walk you home," he says, standing up and reaching down for my hand. His bracelet slides down his wrist and rests against my fingers. We both hop over the rotten step onto the sand. I loosen my fingers on his, just in case he wants to let go of my hand, but he doesn't. We walk toward Gram's, Sam leading the way.

"How do you know where I live?" I ask, even though I already know what he's going to say.

"Small town," he says, squeezing my hand. He walks with me most of the way up the trail to Gram's porch.

"Thanks," I say.

"For what?" he asks.

I shrug a little. "Walking me home." Even though what I want to say is *asking me to the dance, holding my hand, making my night.*

It's only then that I hear her. My mother is standing on the porch, a blanket wrapped around herself.

"Penny," my mother says, "you should come in now." The strain in her voice makes her words clipped.

Marcus takes a step back and I put my hand on his arm. I don't want him to feel guilty about anything.

"Coming." I give Marcus an apologetic smile and say, "See you soon, okay?" before I turn to walk up toward the porch. I know the faster I get inside, the less likely it is that my mother will ruin things completely.

chapter fifteen

I sit on the end of the sofa and pull my knees up into my chest. I was hoping Gram would be here. Maybe to be on my side or maybe just to soften things a little. As if reading my mind, my mother says simply, "She's sleeping." She sits in the straight-back chair near the fireplace, the one Oscar always sleeps in. Oscar threads through her legs, wanting his spot back, then gives up and joins me on the couch.

"I stopped by the bakery tonight after the chamber of commerce meeting." I stare at my feet, noticing that the ankle of one of my socks is gray and speckled. Coffee grounds. "I thought you might like a ride."

"Really," I say, and it comes out nasty, but I don't care.

She pauses for a moment. "I was worried when I couldn't find you."

I just shake my head and look past her.

"Penny . . ." She sighs.

I keep looking past her, as if I'm looking out the window, but it's so dark all I can see is my mother's reflection.

"I know this is hard for you."

"*What* exactly is hard for me?" I ask. My voice is sharp and too loud.

She sighs again. "Starting a new school . . . making new friends . . ."

Say it! I think. Just tell me what I already know. I think about asking her, but I want her to say the words, not just nod in agreement.

Finally she says, "Penny, your father and I are separating."

"What does that mean?" I ask, feeling even more anger rise in me. "Living three hundred miles away from each other already seems pretty separated to me."

She nods and looks at her hands. "Right. But now it's more . . . official." She takes a breath and I wait for more, but she's quiet, maybe waiting for me.

"What now?" I ask.

"I don't know, Penny," she says flatly.

I grab a pillow from the couch and hug it when what I really want to do is punch it. The fact that she doesn't know *what now* is worse than her announcement that they're separating. Without a plan it's pretty obvious. Even though she hasn't used the *D* word yet, unless somebody does something, that's what's next.

When I came inside I thought I was in for a lecture about letting people know where I am or the dangers of being with strange boys in the dark. But instead I get this. We sit for several minutes. I put down the pillow and pet Oscar, feeling him purr.

"Penny—"

I hold up my hand. "If you're going to tell me that you and Dad both love me very much, just don't."

She looks at me for long enough to let me know that was exactly what she was going to say. Now she doesn't know how to go on. Minutes of silence click by on the clock over the mantel.

When she finally does speak again, it's random and weird. "When did you do your hair?"

"A couple of days ago." I reach up and tuck my hair behind my ear again. Tally helped me put highlights in it, so now instead of just plain brown, it looks almost red in the light. I think red was a good choice, better than the green stripes Tally suggested.

"You don't like it," I say, judging by her frown.

"I don't like that it took me a couple of days to see it."

The sadness in her voice takes some of my anger away. There's more I want to talk about, but I don't because she looks too tired and stressed right now.

She keeps starting to say something, but each time she gives up. *I wonder if this awkwardness drove Dad as crazy as it drives me.* I immediately shut down the thought, feeling guilty.

When she finally does speak again, it's just, "Guess I'll head up." She folds her blanket over the back of the chair and walks toward the stairs. "Penny . . ."

She waits for me to look at her, but I don't.

"Don't stay up too late," she says finally.

"I won't," I say. But I'm lying. I know I'll be up most of the night. Sleep seems to be another one of those things I forgot to pack when we moved here.

I'm working the front at the bakery again. It's become my after-school thing. Afternoons are usually pretty slow, so I can get some of my homework done. And boxing up cupcakes and cleaning the glass cases help keep my mind off last night's conversation with my mother.

In between customers, I'm trying to come up with a float design for the parade. I'm the last person who should be working on this. This year's theme is The Way Life Should Be. Right now my life is anything but the way it should be. All I can come up with are suggestions for changing things. I crumple up another piece of paper and lob it toward the trash can.

My mother has been on the phone for most of the afternoon, which is fine with me, because it means we can't have another big talk. I don't know who she's talking to now, but she's obviously not happy with whoever it is. Her voice keeps rising. So much that soon she's going to start hitting an octave only dogs can hear.

Just thinking about dogs makes me think of Sam, and thinking of Sam makes me think of Marcus, and thinking of Marcus makes my heart beat too fast. Half of me is sure he likes me, but only half. Because again today he sat with Charity at lunch. And when he's with her, he won't even look at me. I push my pencil too hard and snap off the point.

I know I'm supposed to be all sophisticated. The big-city girl. But the truth is, Marcus is the first guy I've ever like-liked. Unless you count Tucker in seventh grade, and I don't. Well, I did until he shaved off all his hair, started wearing combat boots, and talked about Warcraft *all the time*.

I keep telling my heart that it shouldn't get all crazy over Marcus, because maybe he's just playing me. Maybe he's even part of Charity's big plan to get back at me. Unfortunately, my heart's not listening very well.

I give up on the float and try to come up with a design for the cupcakes that some woman ordered for her daughter's wedding. *Do something creative!!!* is all that is written below the order details. The many exclamation points tell me it was Gram who took the order. My mom is more of a period woman. I try to think of something new, but it's hard to get all that creative with shades of cream and white.

I lean against the counter and watch the people walking by. Suddenly Tally appears in the front window, waving frantically. I push away from the counter and walk outside.

"What?" I ask, but before I can get out another word, Tally starts talking breathlessly.

"I'm entering—" she says. She's holding a piece of paper, but I can't read it.

Blake runs toward us, his hair flopping with each step. "You have to hurry!" he says. "The form has to be in by five o'clock."

All three of us look at the big clock mounted on the bank building. Five minutes.

"I'll call you," Tally says. Before I can say anything, she's gone.

"What was all that about?" I pull open the door of the bakery to let two women inside.

"Tally is running for Hog Queen," he says.

"What?!"

He shrugs and looks up the street toward where we can just see Tally disappearing into the town hall.

"What possessed her to do that?"

Blake looks as clueless as I feel. "I hope it wasn't anything I said," he says, smiling.

One of the women I just let in peeks around the door and asks me, "Do you work here?" I nod. "I need to order some cupcakes for a baby shower."

"Gotta go," I say to Blake. "I can't wait to hear her explanation for this one."

At least baby shower cupcakes are easy to do when your brain's on overload. I spend the next couple of hours making three dozen cupcakes covered in tiny blue and pink dots, each capped off with an icing bassinet. As I work, the dots seem to spin on the cupcakes, just like all the thoughts in my head. I stop and blink my eyes, trying to focus. It works for the dots, but not so much for everything in my brain.

chapter sixteen

I was hoping Tally would call immediately and fill me in about her decision. After dinner, I finally give up waiting for the phone to ring and walk down to her house.

"Tell me," I say as soon as she opens the door.

Her hair is up in a high twist and skewered with a pencil. She leads me into her kitchen, where she has clothes spread out on all the counters. She picks up a shirt and looks at it.

"Tell me," I say again.

"Okay already!" she says, laughing. "I was helping Poppy hang some of her glass balls in the window of Parlin's store. I'm halfway up a ladder, trying to loop a fishing line over a hook in the ceiling. . . ." Tally looks at me. "That sounds easier than it is. I mean, that fishing line is hard to see and—" Tally stops, seeing my expression. "Anyway, Mrs. Wharton—you know, Charity's mom—comes in and starts blabbing to

Rhonda about how her daughter is a shoo-in for Hog Queen. Blah blah blah." As she parrots Mrs. Wharton, Tally moves her hand like an incredibly lame puppet.

"At what point during all of this did you lose your mind?" I ask.

"Shh," Tally says, pointing the hand puppet at me. "Then—get this—she says: 'Thank you for your contribution to the cash prize.'"

"So?"

"So, I'm thinking that the cash prize would go a long way toward raising money for the ARK. Throw in the added bonus of seeing Charity denied the crown."

"Not to mention the pork products."

"Not to mention. But still, I'm minding my own business, hanging Poppy's witch balls, when suddenly Mrs. Wharton is right there." Tally puts her hand puppet close to her face and then recoils from it. "She starts in on the whole 'Isn't it nice that you're helping Poppy out—considering your situation.'"

"Eww," I say.

"Double eww," Tally agrees. Either Mrs. Wharton is tactless or she's just as mean as her daughter. "Then"—Tally scowls at her hand—"she tells me it's *cute* that I've started my little campaign. *Cute!* Saving animals is not cute." I shake my head in disgust, even though I'm not completely sure why Tally is getting so bent over *cute*. "So that's it," Tally says. She smiles at her hand then shoves it into the front pocket of her hoodie.

"What's it?" I ask.

"That's when I decided. I have officially cast my hat into the ring." Tally flings an imaginary hat onto the floor.

"Are you a hundred percent on this, Tal?" I ask, although I know the answer before she even opens her mouth.

"Hundred and ten," she says. "You're going to help me, right?"

"What about all that subjugation-of-females stuff?"

"Oh, I still totally think pageants are degrading, but I'm not doing it for me, so I can look past the evil machine of modern culture that delivers propaganda to support the value of superficiality."

I nod, trying hard not to laugh.

"Really, I'm not doing it so I can feel okay about myself. I'm solid."

"Okay, then," I say. "What do you want me to do?"

Tally leans against the counter. "Make me more . . ." She pauses and pulls her hair down out of the twist on top of her head. She flips the ends of her hair up to look at them.

"More mainstream?" I ask.

Tally nods. "I mean, Blake says I'm good as is, which earned him some serious brownie points, but I know I'm not exactly what pageant judges go for. I guess I just need to be more . . . more boring." She sighs and tucks her hair behind her ear.

I tilt my head and look at what she's wearing now. Leopard print cat's-eye glasses, green-tipped hair, a skirt that she pieced together out of an old pair of jeans, rainbow-striped leggings, and checkered Vans. "More like me," I say.

Tally considers my jeans and long-sleeved blue T-shirt and smiles. "You are not boring, Penny," she says. "You just keep all of your interesting stuff on the inside."

I shake my head.

Tally picks up a bag from the pharmacy. Through it I can see the outline of a box of hair color. Tally should buy stock in L'Oréal. "Just brown," she says, walking toward the stairs. She turns and looks at me. "Well, come on," she says. "We can talk while we wait for the new color to set." I wonder when was the last time Tally saw her real hair color and if she even remembers what it is.

It's the first time I've ever been in Tally's room. It's weird, too, because if Tally hadn't told me it was hers, I wouldn't have known it. It still looks like someone's den or a guest room. The top of the dresser is bare except for a vase full of dried flowers and a sepia-toned photograph of two very stern-looking people.

"You're quite the minimalist," I say.

Tally looks around her room. "I guess I just haven't really moved in—*considering my situation.*"

"Just ignore her," I say, giving Tally the same advice about Mrs. Wharton that Tally gave me about Charity. Tally goes into the bathroom and closes the door.

I sit on the chair in Tally's room. It's huge, one of those

double papasans that you could fit four people in. It's good that it's big, because I'm sharing it with three of Poppy's now *nine* cats. I hear the sounds of water running and then a box being ripped open.

Petting Mr. Blick, cat number seven, makes me remember petting Oscar during my "talk" with Mom last night. I want to tell Tally what happened, but I'm not up for it yet. I need to figure out how I feel about everything before I talk about it with anyone else.

"So listen," Tally calls from the bathroom. "I have this new theory." I wait for her to continue, but she's quiet again. Finally, the door opens. Tally looks pretty much the same except she's traded her cat's-eye glasses for some bright blue square ones and has her hair bundled on top of her head under a big purple towel. She sits on the bed across from me and puts her hand out.

"New theory?" I wince as Mr. Blick circles in my lap, trying to get comfortable.

"Last night I was messing around online and it occurred to me that RPS is the perfect personality test." She shifts the towel on her head with her spare hand. "Say you throw three papers in a row." I nod and sigh as Mr. Blick finally lies down. "Right away you know you're dealing with someone quiet, but with a lot of confidence."

"Uh-huh," I say, letting Pumpkin rub against my fingers. It's still weird when Tally starts talking about RPS, like at any moment someone is going to pop out of the closet with a camera crew and yell "Gotcha!"

"Each one matches a certain personality type. You know: predictable, unstable, open, closed." Her hand keeps doing the three moves as she talks. I briefly wonder which is a better indicator of personality type, RPS or Jolly Rancher flavors. "You're a bit of a dreamer," Tally says. I start to say something, but she shakes her head and continues. "You're subtle, but with some surprises." She tilts her head slightly, making the towel slip down over one ear. "Maybe a good move for your personality is Paper Dolls," she says. She throws two papers and then a scissor. "Since you're quiet, people might think you'll go for Confetti." She throws three papers in a row. "But that's where you'll fool them."

"How about *your* personality?" I ask, not sure I like being called a dreamer.

"Looking at me, everyone expects that I'll use a combination of scissors and rock." I nod, as if I know what she's talking about. "But lately I've been thinking a lot about chaos theory." Tally looks past my shoulder to the wall clock, made out of an old frying pan. "Be right back," she says. She disappears into the bathroom again, pulling the door shut behind her.

I'm tempted to peek in her closet to see if her belongings are in there, but I don't have the energy. Or maybe I'm just afraid to find out. I lean back and rest my head against the chair. Tally's probably right. Maybe I am just a dreamer. I pinch my arm with my fingers, feeling the sharp bite. Nope.

"Close your eyes," Tally calls from the bathroom.

"Okay," I say, not bothering to tell her they are already shut. I hear the door open, soft footsteps across the wood floor, and then the *shush* of Tally's feet on the rug.

"Okay. Now," Tally says. I open my eyes and Tally is standing in front of me, smiling. "Pretty good, huh?"

"Wow," I say. "You look—"

"Normal?" she asks. She flips her hair slightly. Even though it is still wet, I can tell that it's a deep brown, without a hint of primary color in sight. She's also not wearing glasses anymore.

"Different," I say. Tally walks over to the dresser and turns from side to side to look at her hair in the mirror.

She blinks and rubs at one of her eyes. "Contacts," she says.

I want to tell her that it looks good, but something about seeing Tally suddenly changed makes me sad. It's like each time I get my feet under me, the deck shifts. As much as I want to support Tally's decision to look normal, I could go for a little weird. Somehow, Tally's weird made *me* feel normal.

chapter seventeen

The bell for third period is about to ring, but Tally says she has to tell me something really important and pulls me into the restroom. She makes a big production of peeking under a couple of stalls. I start to mention that I can see a pair of feet under the stall door at the end, but she puts her finger to her lips.

"Okay," she says. Her voice is all excited, but it's false excited, like she's trying out for a play. "I lost five pounds."

"What?" I ask. *Here we go,* I think. Tally is the last person in the world who I expected would be the least bit interested in her weight. She doesn't seem to have any issues with it. I mean, she eats Blake under the table most of the time and yet she's thin. Not yucky model thin, but good thin. Healthy thin.

"I didn't want to tell you until I was sure."

"Sure of what?" I ask. The feet under the last door have stepped forward so far that the toes of the pink plaid ballet flats are sticking all the way out. Whoever is in there would make a terrible spy.

"It all started when I was driving with Poppy to Lancaster," Tally says. She is making her voice go all breathless, and I wonder if this is part of the "new" Tally, the "normal" Tally. "They're doing this story on NPR about alternative medicines. You know, like honey and lemon for sore throats and saline solutions for sinus headaches."

I'm just nodding and watching her. She makes her eyes go big. Okay, now I get the message.

"Uh-huh," I say in a way that I hope matches her false excitement.

"Anyway, they start talking about lard."

"Lard?" I ask. Miss Pink Shoes must be pressed against the door. I can almost feel her holding her breath to listen. "As in pig fat?"

"Yeah," she says. "Apparently, some doctors in Europe have been studying the effects of lard on weight loss." I have to fight to keep a smile from my face. "So anyway," Tally says, making big eyes at me again. *Hold it together,* I think. "All of these models in Europe have started eating lard to keep their weight down. Something about coating your stomach."

"Coating your stomach?" I ask.

"I know," she says. "I didn't believe it either at first, but I went to their Web site. Newlard.com." She says it slowly. "The Web site said that by eating straight animal fat, you overload your system, forcing it to go into emergency mode. It starts dumping all of your fat stores." I can almost see the stall door bow out. "So anyway, I decided to follow the diet. You know, just for a few days, to see if it worked."

"And it did?" I ask.

"Not at first," she says. "I mean, it warns that right on the Web site. That initially, as your body adapts, you will have some bloating."

"Uh-huh," I say.

"And I didn't even do the whole thing. It says for the best results you have to eat straight lard. As much as you can each day. I cheated some and ate those pemmican bars. I mean, that's good—they have lard in them—but for the really good results, you have to do it straight all the way."

"What was the Web site again?" I ask. I pull a pen out of my backpack and pretend to write it on the palm of my hand.

"Newlard.com," Tally says. "I think this is going to be just the key for the pageant," she says. She heads for the door and I follow.

The bell rings as we make it out into the hall. We have to hurry to class to avoid being late. We aren't the only ones, though. I notice that Charlotte is running late, too. She almost trips in the art room as she hurries toward the back table. Someone should warn her that ballet flats can be a little slick on tile floors.

I have to avoid looking at Tally all through class. I'm afraid I'm going to blow it and start laughing. We each keep to ourselves. I work on my float design and Tally is drawing something that looks like a huge sunflower growing out of the planet Saturn. Miss Beans has to keep telling the back table to get to work. They don't stop whispering to one another. I notice that the main person doing the talking is Charlotte, and I notice something else: Charity is listening.

chapter eighteen

*D*ot, dot, line. Line, dot, dot." I have to say the pattern out loud to keep from messing up. I keep blinking, trying to keep my eyes from going out of focus from all of the close work. Forty dozen cupcakes. It's the biggest order we've had yet. It's funny how they always talk about cupcakes that way, in terms of dozens. No one comes in and orders thirty-six cupcakes; it's always three dozen. For the less mathematically inclined, forty dozen = 480. Divide that by the five designs I have to make, and that leaves ninety-six of each kind. I finished the first batch, a Swiss dot pattern, in a couple of hours. The simple shell design and even the more complicated reverse shell took about the same amount of time, but these last two batches are awful. I keep resting my hand because it's cramping so much. The really pathetic part is that my mother isn't even here to help. Normally she would at least help with the decorating. She had to go to some meeting in the

City and won't be back until late. Way too late to do much more than drop into bed and then get up early to deliver the cupcakes out to the beach for the dawn wedding. I keep hoping that all these meetings are maybe going to change things. It seems like as long as everything is still in the air, there's still some hope.

"So you should come by the ARK one Saturday," Tally says. "We open at nine for adoption."

"I have to ask Gram," I say for the hundredth time.

"She'll say yes," Tally says. She's probably right. Gram probably will say yes, but I still have to ask. "I know," Tally says, spinning to look at me, "bring her with you. Then she'll be sure to say yes."

I nod and start the next cupcake.

"Just say yes to Tally," Blake says. "She won't stop until you do."

"Marcus will be there," she says. "He's always there on Saturdays."

If I needed any more convincing, that was it. "Okay," I say, pretending to be a little annoyed. "Yes." *Dot. Dot. Line.* "Tell me again why you think Charity is going to go for it." *Line. Dot. Dot.* "She's not fat," I say.

"She's fourteen and she has to walk across a stage in a bathing suit," Tally says.

"Maybe," I say. "But why would she trust anything we say? I mean, she hates us."

"I'm betting that Charlotte's not going to share the source of her information. She is going to tell Charity that she heard it on the radio and she checked the Web site."

I nod, agreeing. That much is pretty sure. Charlotte is always following Charity around like a lost puppy. Having the inside scoop on something would make her seem more important in Charity's eyes.

"The Web site's pretty lame," I say. I smile over at Tally.

She shrugs and smiles back. "That's what you get for seventy-five dollars," she says.

"You have to admit that the success stories are pretty good, though," Blake says. He and his brother, some sort of computer genius, put the whole thing together. The money was for buying server space.

"They're totally over-the-top. Fifteen pounds in two weeks?" I ask.

"It has to be over-the-top," Tally says. "It has to promise big results. Otherwise she might not go for it."

"When will we know?" I ask.

"I predict that by Monday there's going to be a rash of lard purchases at the Shop 'n Save."

I shake my head and look back down at the cupcake in front of me. Lard. Yuck.

"Tell me the stuff in the can isn't lard," I say, thinking of the spoonfuls of goop she's been eating every day.

"It's vanilla frosting," she says. "It's not as bad as lard, but pretty gross anyway." I nod. That's one thing about working at the bakery, you get pretty sick of sweet stuff. I keep piping, trying to stay on track.

"Who gets married at dawn?" Blake asks, tucking more cupcakes into one of the big pink boxes.

"I think it's romantic," Tally says.

"Romantic is getting enough sleep." Blake keeps putting cupcakes into the boxes, avoiding eye contact with Tally.

"Remind me to get you an I HEART SLEEP shirt for Valentine's Day," Tally says.

I put the pastry bag down and shake out my hand again. Tally looks over and frowns. "I wish we could help more with that."

I shrug and smile. They helped with the first coat of frosting, but I have to do the fussy decorating work myself. "I'm going to need more buttercream soon," I say, twisting the pastry bag a bit to make sure all of the icing is forced toward the tip. Blake and Tally both touch their noses at almost the same time.

Gram comes into the kitchen from the front, wiping her hands on the towel tucked into her apron string. "Why are we touching our noses?" she asks.

"Last one to touch has to make buttercream," I say.

"Are we out?" Gram asks, pulling the refrigerator door open. She opens a big plastic storage tub and shakes her head.

Blake is still standing with his index finger on his nose. Tally sighs. "I'll make it," she says. "Just tell me what to do."

I start rattling off the recipe. If I had to guess, I'd say I've made about three hundred batches of buttercream since I've been here. That's in addition to the fudge and cream cheese icing, and the mountains of whipped cream I've made. I keep decorating, mumbling the pattern under my breath while Tally starts stirring the mixture of egg whites and sugar over the double boiler on the stove.

"I'm going for pizza," Gram says, pulling her jacket on. "Any requests?" We each throw in some suggestions. Tomatoes and spinach for me. Mushrooms and extra cheese for Blake. Tally wants pineapple. She winks at Blake when she says it, and he smiles. Gram pulls the back door shut behind her and then I hear her Volvo wagon start up.

Tally keeps stirring the mixture on the stove, trying to get the sugar to dissolve completely. "Hey, Rip Van Winkle," she says. "Can you get some butter out of the fridge for me?"

Blake walks over and rummages in the refrigerator for a few moments. "Where is it?" he asks. Tally sighs and walks over to where he's standing. She starts pushing things aside.

"It's in the big brown box on the bottom," I say. Tally pulls the box out and upends it over the floor. Empty. I hold up the almost empty pastry bag. "This isn't enough."

"Call the dairy," Blake says. We all look at the clock. Seven-thirty. "Probably not."

Tally walks toward the desk in the back and picks up the phone book. In Manhattan there were four huge volumes of numbers. Here it's barely the size of a magazine.

"What is she doing?" I ask Blake.

He shrugs. "You'll learn not to ask," he says.

She pokes some numbers into the phone and waits. She starts talking. All I hear is mumbling and then a laugh. She turns and looks at me while she talks. "Done and done," she says, pushing the *Off* button on the phone. "Someone from the dairy will be here in about ten," she says. She goes back over to the stove and scrapes the bottom of the bowl again, folding the sticky mixture. "You might want to go and freshen up a bit."

"Why?" I ask. I look over at Blake, who is shaking his head and making a slicing gesture across his neck.

"Don't ask," he says in an exaggerated whisper.

"Trust me," Tally says. She laughs right after she says it, which doesn't exactly inspire confidence. But I put down my pastry bag anyway and head for the bathroom.

For me, freshening up consists of washing off the blob of buttercream that somehow made its way onto my cheek and making my ponytail less chaotic. Against Blake's advice I did ask Tally why I should care about what I look like, but she just shook her head at me and smiled. I feel foolish cleaning up for the dairy delivery. It's usually either this old guy named Gus, who always *always* calls me Patti, or this woman who constantly pops her cinnamon gum while I check the order.

"Better?" I ask, walking back out into the kitchen. Blake is standing with Tally at the stove. He has his chin on her shoulder, and she is leaning into him. They spring apart at the sound of my voice. I notice that Blake even blushes on the top of his head. It's weird sometimes how they are, all teasing and jokey when other people are around, but then so sweet to each other when they think no one can see.

"Let's see," Tally says, making a circle with her finger. I spin slowly. She nods and reaches into her pocket. "Here," she says, tossing me a tin of Altoids.

"Tal, what is going on?" I ask. I hear the sound of a motor in the alley behind the bakery, but it's not loud enough to be either the dairy truck or Gram's wagon.

"Hold that thought," Tally says. I look over at Blake, but he won't meet my eyes. He just keeps smiling into the bakery box that he's filling. I hear the back door open and then Tally's voice saying, "Come in, come in." She rounds the corner, followed by someone carrying a huge box of butter. *Marcus.* "Put it anywhere," she says, then laughs slightly. Every spare surface is covered with half-filled boxes of cupcakes. Tally clears a small corner of the desk.

"Hi," Marcus says, smiling at me. He puts the box down. Tally immediately starts ripping into the box and hauling out several pounds of butter.

"Hi." I'm probably blushing more than Blake did. "Thank you so much," I say, gesturing toward the box of butter. I notice that Marcus is blushing a little, too. It seems that only Tally is immune to embarrassment. She just hums as she starts pouring the buttercream base into the huge Hobart mixer. I help her put the whisk on.

"What can I do?" Marcus asks.

"Oh, you don't have to—" I begin.

"Maybe he wants to," Tally whispers, elbowing me.

"Maybe I want to," Marcus says, smiling.

"You can help box cupcakes," I say, pointing to where Blake is trying to put the tops on some of the boxes before sliding them into the refrigerator.

"Yeah. I could use an assistant," Blake says.

Tally rolls her eyes at him. "Okay, Blake, you've been working here for an hour. I'm pretty sure we'll be starting Marcus off at the same level."

Marcus washes his hands and pulls an apron off one of the hooks in the back so he is outfitted like the rest of us. "Just tell me what to do," he says.

I have to study the cupcake in front of me to remind myself where I am in the pattern. *Dot, dot, line. Marcus. Line, dot, dot. Like me as much as I like you.*

Gram comes in carrying two large pizzas. The smell immediately makes my mouth water.

"Yum," Blake says, starting for the first box.

"Not until you're done," Tally says, her voice sounding just like Blake's when we were picking tomatoes.

With Gram helping me decorate, Tally turning out another batch of buttercream, and Marcus and Blake boxing, the remaining cupcakes go quickly. "Last one," I say, poking the final silver ball onto the last cupcake.

"Sweet," Blake says, placing it into the box and taping the top shut. We don't bother to clean up right away. Instead we fall onto the pizza, all of us eating like we haven't had any food in a month. Blake manages to put away almost a whole pizza all by himself. "I have only two words for that," he says, leaning back against the shelves behind him. "Goo-ood." Tally just shakes her head, but she leans into him slightly, so that her shoulder is against his. After only a little bit of convincing, Tally gets Gram to agree to come to the ARK with me. Blake pushes the last bite of crust into his mouth. "Who's up for dessert?" he asks. Even Gram groans at that one.

It takes a while to clean up. Not only do we have to wash all of the equipment and make sure everything is properly boxed and labeled and put away, but we also have to mop the floor. Blake loses at RPS to Tally in a best of three out of five. He gets stuck with the floor, while Tally and I start washing out the pastry bags.

"So, Marcus," Blake says, his back to us, "how's your knee coming along?" I look over at Marcus, who is struggling to wash out the big mixing bowl.

"It's better," he says to Blake. "Why? You worried?"

Tally sees the expression on my face. "Soccer," she says, and rolls her eyes. I start washing the decorating tips, using a skewer to get the icing out of their tiny ends. I half listen as Marcus and Blake talk about the upcoming season. They both played forward on rival teams all summer. Marcus's team won the final. Blake's got second place.

"Saw you on the field yesterday," Blake says.

Marcus turns to look at him. "When?" His voice sounds funny. Tense.

Blake shrugs. "Four-ish. Didn't know *she* played soccer." His voice sounds weird, too, almost hostile.

I feel my stomach twist, thinking about Charity alone with Marcus on the soccer field. I look over at where Blake is leaning on the mop. Tally looks up, too, but Blake won't meet our eyes. Marcus keeps scrubbing the bowl, but the back of his neck is red.

"So, what's the deal?" Blake asks. Tally shakes her head at him, but he doesn't seem to notice.

"Nothing," Marcus says. "There's no deal." He finishes with the bowl and turns to me. I can't tell whether he's angry or embarrassed or if his cheeks are just flushed from the steam coming off the water in the sink. "Want me to take the trash out to the Dumpster?" he asks, nodding toward the two bags waiting by the back door.

"Sure." He walks over and opens the door, picking up both bags in one hand.

When he is out of earshot, Tally asks Blake, "What was that all about?"

Blake goes back to mopping. "Just telling him what's up."

"What are you talking about?" Tally asks.

Blake looks over at me. "Just making sure he knows I've got my eye on him." He points to his eye and then to the door. He goes back to mopping. I look over at Tally, but she just shrugs.

Marcus comes back in before any of us can say anything else.

No one says anything to him for a moment. "Thank you again for helping," I say to him, breaking the silence.

"It was fun," he says, untying his apron.

"Anyone need a ride?" Gram asks, coming back into the kitchen from the front.

I'm about to say yes, but Tally elbows me and says, "I think we're good." Gram winks at me before heading out, with reminders to lock up when we leave. We finish up quickly and trade our aprons for our jackets.

"Okay, then," Tally says, stepping out onto the back porch. I flick the lights off and pull the door shut behind me, hearing the lock click into place. "Marcus, can you give Penny a ride home?"

"It's okay," I say. "I can walk."

"Maybe he wants to," Tally says in an exaggerated whisper.

"Maybe I want to," Marcus says, smiling.

chapter nineteen

*M*arcus takes a second helmet from the compartment under the seat of his four-wheeler. Either this was planned or he's used to riding with somcone else. But I'm not going to think about that and ruin a perfectly good night. Before I can thank them for everything, Tally and Blake are riding off side by side on their mountain bikes. I can hear Tally laughing even as they make their way around the corner onto Main Street.

"You ready?" Marcus asks. I pull on a helmet and climb on behind him, aware of how close we are. "Hang on," he says. I look for somewhere to put my hands. "To me," he says softly. It's good that it's so dark. I'm pretty sure I'm hitting a personal best for blushing. The four-wheeler rumbles under us as Marcus starts it up. I slide my hands around his waist, feeling his warmth beneath his fleece coat. "Do you have to go straight home, or do you want to go see something first?" he asks.

"I've got time," I say. *I'll go see anything with you,* I'm thinking. *I don't care what it is.*

We steer out onto Main Street and slide past the darkened shops, past the clock tower with its face lit up. We go farther, past the turnoff for the beach and out to where the edge of town gives way to apple orchards and the rolling fields of the pig farms. We slow down and Marcus turns us off the main road and onto a dirt road almost invisible in the trees.

"Hang on," he says again, taking his hand off the handlebars for a moment and touching my arms. "It gets a little bumpy up ahead." I pull in a little closer, pressing my cheek into the middle of his back, and breathing in the smell that is all but gone from the sweatshirt that I still have at home. But now his smell is layered with the scents from the bakery. "It's just up here," he says. We both lean forward as he steers the four-wheeler uphill. The cold wind bites at us, making me shiver a little. "Can you see it now?" Marcus asks. I lean out to the side to look around him. I start to ask what I'm looking for, but then I see it. An enormous ball of some kind, just a dark shadow against the night sky.

"It's huge," I say. "What is it?"

"Just wait," Marcus says. "You'll see." The road veers to the right, taking us past some trees that temporarily obscure the ball. The road curves again, this time to the left, and we go right up to the base of the object. It's even bigger than I thought. As big as a truck or a minivan—maybe bigger. I can see from this side that it's only half of a ball. The inside is a huge web of wire and beams. It's supported on four metal poles, each maybe six feet tall.

"It's beautiful," I say. The closer I look, the more I see. It's actually pieced together out of several metals, each a slightly different color. Marcus turns off the motor and douses the headlight. We don't need it—the clearing is bright enough in the light of the full moon. And the cool, almost blue light of the moon seems to make the colors of the sphere stand out even more than the yellow light of the headlight. We pull off our helmets. I climb off the four-wheeler and walk around toward the finished side of the ball. "Can I touch it?" I ask.

"Of course," Marcus says, walking toward me. I have to stand on my tiptoes to reach even the bottom of the ball. It's cool to the touch as I run my fingers lightly over one of the seams between colors. I step back slightly and look at the face of it. A huge reddish patch stares out at me from close to the bottom of the sphere.

"It looks like an . . . eye," I say. Suddenly I realize what this is. "Jupiter," I say. I look over at Marcus. He smiles at me and then looks back at the planet. "It's amazing. Who—?"

"My dad," Marcus says. "Well, and me a little, but all I do is haul materials and hold things while he's welding."

All I can think of is what Blake told me about Mr. Fish trying to contact aliens. For a second I wonder if he was right.

I step back and look again. "It's really amazing," I say. Marcus smiles. "Have you done any of the other planets?" I ask.

Marcus nods and steps close to me. He points off into the distance, toward one of the hills. "If you look closely, you can see Venus from here." I look where he is pointing, at first frustrated that I can't see it, then it's there. A yellow ball way in the distance. "The rest are scattered around us in the hills. They're all hidden in the trees. You can see the edge of Neptune from here in the daytime, but it's too dark now. The others are too far to see."

"The others?" I ask. "Does all this land belong to you?"

Marcus laughs and shakes his head. "No, all of this is state forest," he says. "My dad had to get all sorts of permits and inspections. They finally let him because he convinced them that it was 'a value-adding project.'" He looks over at me and laughs at the look on my face. "Their words, not mine. Pretty much, Dad just got lucky. The state senator is a space nut."

"I guess I'm a nut, too," I say. "Because this is one of the most beautiful things I've ever seen." I look back at the face of Jupiter, tracing the bands of color with my eyes.

"There are three kinds of copper," Marcus says. "And steel and aluminum." He points to each stripe as he speaks. "It was hard finding the red. My dad had to special order it from a foundry in upstate New York."

"And it's just the two of you doing this?" I ask. Marcus looks away, but not before I see his eyes get shiny.

"I'm sorry," I say. "I didn't mean to—"

Marcus turns back to me. "You didn't," he says. "It's just still hard to talk about." He walks around the side of Jupiter, toward a huge rock that is suspended above a drop-off. He sits, dangling his legs over the edge. I sit beside him, and we look out toward the hills and beyond, where the water is lit by the moon.

"It was my mom," he says, looking down at his feet swinging high over the trees below us. "She was the one who had the idea to build all this. She was really into it, mapping it all out, dragging me up here all the time to put in these stakes with purple ribbons tied to them." He looks at me, his eyes still sad. "It's all to scale," he says. "One mile equals one astrological unit." He smiles at the confusion on my face. "Earth is one astrological unit or ninety-three million miles from the sun. Pluto is forty astrological units from the sun."

"So, you can't see her Pluto from here," I say.

Marcus smiles and shakes his head. "Not without a really good telescope."

"Your mom was an astronomer?" I ask.

"Amateur. She was actually an English teacher, but she loved astronomy. Anything about stars or planets. She was crazy for it."

"I can see why," I say, looking back at Jupiter.

He slides closer to me and nudges my foot with his. He gazes back out over the hills. "When my mom died, my dad went kind of nuts. He'd walk the beach all day, come in to sleep for a few hours, then he'd be back out there again. It was like he couldn't get enough of the beach. And then one day he was just done. He hasn't been back since. He turned to this instead."

"How long has he been working on it?" I ask.

"Over a year." Marcus looks at my face and smiles slightly. "I know. He's out here almost all the time. If he's not at the dairy, he's here. If he's not here or at the dairy, he's asleep."

"That must be hard," I say, feeling guilty about how I've been thinking about my mom. At least she hasn't completely lost it.

Marcus shrugs. "This is better than the walking. At least he's doing something."

And maybe he's right. Maybe creating all of this has given him something to grab onto. "Building this must make him feel closer to her," I say. Something about tonight is making me say things that I would normally just keep to myself.

Marcus nods. "It does. It gives him something to do, not just feel."

"It's a pretty awesome tribute." I think about the kind of love that inspires people to do great things. Beautiful things. I can't imagine either of my parents being so devoted.

Marcus looks out over the trees and says almost to himself, "I hope she can see them."

"Well, they're certainly big enough," I say playfully. I worry a little bit that he'll think I'm making fun of him, but then he chuckles softly. "How many more do you have to build?" I ask.

"Just this one and Saturn." He looks out toward a hill to our left. "He's probably out at the Saturn site tonight. He's been clearing brush there for the last couple of days."

"He's almost done, then."

"Yeah," Marcus says softly. "That's what I'm worried about."

I look back at Jupiter again. The moonlight reflecting off the different metals makes them seem to glow. "I bet he'll be fine. I bet this has made both of you stronger."

"Yeah, you should feel my muscles," he says, his eyes crinkling.

Now it's my turn to chuckle. But this time I don't say what I'm thinking: *I would love to!*

Marcus reaches over and loops his pinkie finger over mine. We sit like that, just our pinkies linked, looking out over the trees to where the water meets the sky.

"I should probably get home," I say, finally. I don't want to worry Gram, who I am sure is waiting up both to make sure I'm safe and to see if she can get any details about Marcus.

"I should probably get back, too," he says, pushing himself up to standing. He extends his hand and helps me up. "Thank you for tonight," he says, still holding my hand as we walk over to where the four-wheeler is parked.

"You're welcome," I say, but it seems weird, because I feel like I should be thanking *him*. I'm grateful he trusted me enough to bring me here. Trusted me enough to tell me about his mom. For the first time since I've been here, I feel connected, and not just to Marcus, but to everything. I can understand why people say this place is where life is like it should be. No bright lights and pretty wrappings, just life with its sadness and its happiness all mixed together.

I pull my helmet on and climb on behind Marcus. He squeezes my hand again before turning on the engine. "Hang on," he says, but this time he doesn't need to, because I'm already hanging on—tight.

chapter twenty

*M*iss Beans says that to get better at something, you have to do it every day. She doesn't care what you draw, just that you do. A sketch a day. So far this week I've drawn the view of the beach from Gram's house; one of Poppy's witch balls; Oscar asleep in the window seat in the kitchen; and my foot. In art on Fridays, once we turn in our sketchbooks for the week, we can work on our other projects. I'm fiddling with my float design, but I keep getting distracted by thoughts of Marcus. Luckily, by the time he dropped me off last night, my mother had already disappeared into her bedroom. I just wanted to float along for a bit without her sending me crashing back to Earth.

I glance over at Tally, who is trying to finish three days' worth of sketches in one class period. This is the first time I've been able to talk to her without Blake around. I think I already know the answer, but I have to ask. "What was Blake talking about with Marcus at the bakery?"

Tally stops drawing and looks over at me. She pauses for a moment, like she's considering what to say.

"Just tell me," I say.

"Blake said he saw Charity with Marcus at the soccer field."

"Oh," I say, pretending to study my drawing. "That's what I thought."

"He said she was just standing around watching him."

"Still . . . ," I say.

Tally squints her eyes at me. "Forget about it. It's obvious he's totally into you."

I smile down at my paper. "Maybe," I say. It helps to hear Tally confirm it. We couldn't both be wrong, could we?

"Besides," Tally says, "Blake put him on notice." She mimics Blake's weird hand gestures, pointing first to her eye and then toward the door. She is so good at imitating his intense look that I start giggling. Miss Beans looks over at us, making me laugh even more.

Tally tries to peek at my work. "Stop," I mouth at her, hunching over my paper to block her view. She just smiles and winks at me. Today she's wearing a navy blue sweater and a short skirt with ballet flats. Her plain brown hair is pulled back from her face with a blue-and-green-plaid headband. It's weird how she's completely bought into this whole pageant thing. I know she said it's for the ARK, but she seems to be enjoying it, too. I squint over at her. "Are you wearing lipstick?" I ask. She makes her eyes go big and tries to peek at my paper again. "Stop," I say. She smiles again but goes back to her own drawing. I have my basic float design sketched out. I just want to add a little color before I turn it in. I shade the tomatoes red, adding green leaves for contrast.

"Come to the library with me after lunch," Tally says. "I have to show you what I've added to the Web site."

"Can't," I say. "I have to go see Madame Framboise."

"Why?" Tally asks.

"Apparently I'm not doing so well in French."

"*Poisse,*" Tally says.

I nod. Bummer is right. The bell rings just as I am finishing the shading on the sprinkles.

"Okay, let me see," Tally says. She walks behind me and looks over my shoulder. "Whoa," she says. "It's really good. Random, but good." I slide it into the manila envelope Miss Beans gave me.

"Now I just wait." I reach down and pick up the rest of my books. Tally follows me to the door, where I add my envelope to the growing stack in Miss Beans's box. We walk to my locker first. I spin the lock and pull it open.

"They're just getting lame," I say, reaching in. I take out the carton of sour milk and drop it in the trash. "It's like they're not even trying anymore."

"What was it last time?" Tally asks.

"Shaving cream." That took me a while to clean up. "Maybe they think to get better at it, they have to do it every day."

This makes Tally laugh. "They'll get tired of it eventually. I told you. Just act like you don't care."

I nod and pull out my lunch and click the locker shut. I stopped requesting new lockers when I realized that somehow they were able to find out the combination within a day or so of me switching. Plus they told me in the office they'd run out of empty lockers.

"Besides," Tally says, "if you act disinterested, they won't suspect our evil plans." She rubs her hands together in an imitation of a movie villain.

We head to the lunchroom and toward our table. I figure I'll eat fast and then go see Madame Framboise. At least then if the news is really bad, I can take it on a full stomach. As we walk past where Charity and her friends are sitting, we notice that almost all of them have a cup of sticky-looking white stuff on the table in front of them. I have to hand it to Tally. She nailed it. For over two weeks now they've been at it, sucking down cup after cup of lard. Charity is the worst, though. She even got caught sneaking some in science class, earning herself a detention. Just to make sure no one bails on the diet, Tally and I've been holding our covert meetings in the bathroom, giving each other our diet reports, telling each other to hang in there. That the bloating is temporary. Charlotte must be living in the restroom, because every time we go in there, she's holed up in the last stall. An added bonus is that we've noticed that there seems to be a weird pimple epidemic among Charity's gang.

"I didn't even think about the zit factor, but I should have seen that one coming," Tally says. "You can't eat that much fat without your body starting to do weird things." Tally and I sit at our table, where Blake is already halfway through his second sandwich. Peanut butter and grape jelly. No lard. He's completely immersed in some thick paperback with a dragon on the cover. He nods at us when we sit down, then goes right back to reading. I look over to where Marcus is sitting with the rest of the soccer players. He's laughing at the guy sitting across from him, who has a straw stuck up his nose.

Tally sees them, too. "Boys are so stupid," she says. She glances at Blake when she says it, but he doesn't even look up from his book.

I stare down at my sandwich. I wish I had the nerve to go over and talk to him, but I don't. Right now he's the *other* Marcus, the school Marcus. He doesn't even look my way when I throw out my garbage in the can closest to him. I don't get it. I thought last night would change things.

Madame Framboise is sitting at her desk when I walk into the room. She's eating a sandwich and reading a magazine. It's always so weird when you see teachers doing normal things, like when you run into them at the grocery store. I just don't want to know that my teacher likes Nutter Butters and Eezy Cheez.

"Penny," she says, flipping the magazine closed and putting it facedown on the desk. She dusts off her hands and lifts a file folder from her desk. "I'm glad you stopped by." Teachers are always saying stuff like that. Like I had a choice. "I know you've been really struggling this semester. Before things head south, I think we should consider tutoring." She flips through the file in front of her, pulls out a sheet, and hands it to me. I scan the names and phone numbers on the list. I recognize a few names—juniors and seniors mostly. She leans forward and taps the first name on the list. "This is who I would recommend. She's quite fluent, and I think she could really help you grasp the subtleties of the language." She sits back and looks at me.

"Thank you," I say. "I mean, *merci*." I slide the list into the front of my notebook. "I really appreciate you suggesting this."

The bell signaling the end of lunch rings as I step into the hall. I do think tutoring is a good idea. I'm just not so sure about Madame's choice of tutors. Even if she is fluent in French, I don't think Charity would be a good match for me.

Tired of being passive, I decide to walk up to Jupiter. Of course, I need a reason to go, so I enlisted Gram's help. First I borrowed a book from the library with photographs of all the planets.

"I can't believe they decided Pluto wasn't a planet after all," Gram says. She's been mixing icing colors for me for half an hour. There are a lot of different colors in our solar system. "So one day Pluto's up there, floating around, minding his own business, and he gets the call that he's been demoted."

I laugh at the image of Pluto with a phone to his ear, looking shocked. "I'd be mad," I say.

"That kind of news should be delivered in person," she says, adding a few more drops of food coloring to the royal blue she's been making. "Speaking of phone calls . . ."

"Were we?" I ask. Gram isn't the best at being subtle when she has something on her mind.

"Have you spoken to your father recently?" she asks.

That makes me stop smiling. "We've been e-mailing."

"That's not the same as talking," she says. "And I can't say you've been communicating much with your mother, either."

I have to force myself not to shake my head at her. I don't know which is worse, hearing what they have to tell me, or not hearing what they should be telling me.

When I don't say anything, Gram continues to push it. "You can't avoid them forever, you know." She walks around the table and rubs my back. "I know I sound like a nosy old lady, but I'm just worried about you. If you continue to keep it all bottled up, you might explode someday."

I can feel tears coming on, so I take a deep breath before

saying, "Could I finish decorating these cupcakes before we talk? This one's kind of tricky. . . ."

It looks like Gram isn't going to let me off the hook that easily, but just then the bells on the front door jingle. She goes to wait on the customer, leaving me to navigate the solar system alone.

There are ten cupcakes in all. One sun, eight planets, and Pluto. I thought about making a couple of the moons to round out the dozen, but I ran out of time. Besides, I kind of like that I am the first person to take a box of just ten cupcakes and not some fraction or combination of a dozen. The walk up to Jupiter isn't bad. It only takes me a little over half an hour from the bakery. I hear the crackle of the blowtorch even before I can see the top of the dome.

Mr. Fish is perched on the top of the metal scaffolding. He looks down at me and raises a gloved hand. I smile, not wanting to try to balance the box of cupcakes in one hand.

Marcus waves to me when he spots me at the edge of the clearing. "Hey, what are you doing here?" he asks when I walk up.

"I was just in the neighborhood," I say.

"Uh-huh," he says. He smiles at me, and I exhale a little. I was nervous during the whole walk from the bakery. I can't seem to predict which Marcus is going to show up. The friendly-flirty one who smiles a lot, or the distant one, who will barely meet my eyes. "Can you help me for a minute?" he asks. He drags a heavy piece of pipe across to where his father is working.

"Just tell me what to do," I say, smiling as I remember Marcus saying the same thing to me at the bakery. I put the cupcakes down on a cooler. I want to give them to him when he's not so busy.

Marcus hands me a pair of gloves. He lifts a huge, square piece of copper out of a pile and hands it to me. "Careful. The edges are sharp. Just take that over to my dad." I start to walk over to where Mr. Fish is working. "Oh, and don't look directly at the blowtorch. It'll hurt your eyes."

I wait at the base of the scaffolding, feeling the heat from the sparks even though they're falling several feet away from me. Mr. Fish douses the flame and lifts his visor.

"Hey there, ghost girl," he says. He climbs down a level, and I hand up the piece of copper. "Thanks," he says, taking it from me. "Tell Marcus this is it for tonight." He flips his visor down and relights his torch. I watch for a moment as he carefully connects the piece of copper to the one below it, sealing the edges together until it almost looks like it grew that way. Now, like the pine trees and aspen all around us, Jupiter just belongs here.

I walk back over to Marcus, who is peeking into the box. He looks up at me sheepishly. "Sorry," he says. "I do the same thing at Christmas. It used to drive my mom nuts." He smiles a little as he says it, but it's the sad one that doesn't quite make it up to his eyes. He sits on a log, still holding the box of cupcakes. "Can I have one?" he asks.

"Have 'em all," I say. "I made them specifically for you."

"Really?" he says, with little-boy happiness, as if it *is* Christmas.

I sit down on the other end of the log. "Your dad says he's almost done."

Marcus nods and looks up to where his dad is climbing down the ladder. Then he pulls at the tape on the box, opening it up all the way. "Wow," he says. "These are amazing."

"They aren't to scale," I say. "One astronomical unit does not equal one sprinkle."

Marcus laughs. I like his laugh, and the way his eyes crinkle when he does. I make a note to try and make him laugh more often.

"How did you make the rings?" he asks, lifting Saturn out of the box.

"Pulled sugar," I say. What I don't tell him is that the rings took nearly as long to make as all the other cupcakes put together.

"You must have spent hours on these," Marcus says.

I say softly, "It was worth it." *Just to see that crinkle again,* I think.

Mr. Fish walks over to where we are sitting. Marcus shows him the cupcakes. "Wow," Mr. Fish says. "You're a real artist, Penny." He takes Jupiter out of the box, holds it up toward the big Jupiter above us, and smiles. I shrug. "No, really," he says. "I'm beginning to think there's something in the water around here. Seems like everyone's an artist."

I'm not sure what to say. I've never thought of myself that way. I just like to make things that make people happy. I've never thought of it as art before.

"They're too pretty to eat," he says.

I hear a crunch beside me and look over to see Marcus with half of Saturn's rings hanging from his mouth. He looks a little sheepish again, but I notice it doesn't stop him from taking a bite out of the planet itself.

Mr. Fish returns Jupiter to the box. "I think I'll save mine until after dinner." He raises an eyebrow at Marcus, who just smiles with sprinkles in his teeth. Mr. Fish smiles back, shaking his head. "I'm going to load up," he says. He picks up the cooler and his visor and walks down the trail to where the truck is parked.

Alone with Marcus, I suddenly feel nervous again. I want to ask him what's going on, why he seems to be two people, but suddenly Blake's voice is in my head: *When I hang out with guys, I just chill.* I try to just chill, but I'm not very good at it. Finally, I just ask him about soccer. I listen, nodding the whole time, still trying to figure out how to ask what I really want to know about—Charity.

"Will you look at that," Mr. Fish says, walking back up the hill. I look toward where he is pointing, out past the hills, in time to see the sun just dipping into the water. We all watch as the huge red ball slowly sinks into the ocean.

"Now *that's* what I'd call art," I say.

"I'll eat to that," Marcus says, and reaches in for his second cupcake. I watch as he does his own bit to extinguish the sun.

chapter twenty-one

*T*he bakery is quiet because of the rain. It keeps seeping under the front door. Every ten minutes or so I have to use towels to try to sop up the water. Normally the awning might keep the rain from even hitting the sidewalk out front, but the wind is blowing so hard, the water is coming at us almost sideways.

"First big storm of the year," Gram says, coming out of the back to stock the display case with more fall-themed cupcakes. I made the expected: jack-o'-lanterns, colored leaves, scarecrows (stuffed with toasted coconut instead of straw). My favorites are the ones with a horn of plenty on top. They are fussy, with all of the tiny fruit coming out of the chocolate horns, but they are the best sellers. Someone from the City called and ordered three dozen for a party they're having in a couple of weeks, so in between trying to stop the flood coming under the door, I'm rolling tiny squashes and apples and even tinier grapes out of colored marzipan.

"Penny," my mom calls from the back. I wipe the powdered sugar from my hands on the towel tucked into my apron. I take a deep breath and push through the door to the kitchen. *Here we go.* I've been working up the courage to talk to her all morning. I know what Gram said yesterday was right. We can't avoid each other forever, especially after Dad's latest e-mail. But each time I get up my nerve, the phone rings, or the puddle gets big again, or . . .

My mother is bent over her calendar, which is laid out across the big worktable in the kitchen. She looks up when I come in.

"Mom," I say, "I think we need to talk." I take a breath, then another. I'm not sure how to begin. Do I ask about the meetings in the City she keeps going to? She looks at me, waiting. "I'm just not sure about the Thanksgiving orders," I say, wimping out.

She nods slowly. I think she knows that's not really what I wanted to talk about. She pauses for a moment before looking back down at the calendar. "I'm thinking we need to cut things off. It's really starting to fill up. With all the traffic going past the shop because of the festival, this might be all I can handle. As it is, I know I'm really imposing on you."

I walk around and look at the two weeks going into Thanksgiving. "It is a lot," I say.

"Penny," she says, "I want you to know that I really appreciate all of your help." She looks up at me, and I take a deep breath, but as if on cue, the phone does ring. My mom picks it up and turns away from me to talk. I try giving myself a little pep talk. *I can do this. It's my own mother. What's the big deal?* "Of course. I'll be here all afternoon. See you then." My mom puts the phone down. "That was Tally. She's stopping by."

"Didn't she want to talk to me?" I ask.

My mom's cheeks go pink. "Actually, she wanted to talk to *me.*" I raise my eyebrows. "About the pageant." *Great. Tally can talk to my mom no problem. Me? I'm a mess.* "She wanted to know if I could give her some advice." Mom leans against the counter. "I don't think I ever told you." She shifts slightly and won't meet my eyes. "I was Hog Queen."

"Really," I say, a little frustrated. This isn't the talk we are supposed to be having.

She nods and looks up at me. These days, instead of just being distant, she seems sort of fragile. It's weird seeing her like this. She's no longer the unshakable Mom. The one who can juggle her own business and still make time for weekend picnics and staying up all night with me to make a volcano out of plaster and paint. But she's not a totally broken one either. She's both.

"Tell me about it," I say.

She smiles. The first real smile I've seen in forever. "There was this one time I almost set my hair on fire, thinking I could twirl a flaming baton." She sees the look on my face and laughs. "It was pretty exciting. They had to douse me with the fire extinguisher."

"But you still won," I say.

She nods and shrugs. "It did leave an impression on the judges."

She keeps talking. Gram walks back into the kitchen when she hears us laughing and starts adding her own memories. The talent stuff is the best. Trained pigs, and hula hoops, and even burping. Gram and Mom can barely stop laughing when they tell me that one.

"She made it all the way to *Q*," Gram says, wiping her eyes with the edge of her apron. I try to imagine a girl in a fancy dress belching the alphabet.

Tally arrives with her arms full of dresses she picked up at the secondhand store in Lancaster. We all take turns going out front to mop up the water still coming in under the door while Tally starts her own mini fashion show, donning dress after dress to show my mother. We keep the ovens going, baking cupcakes as we talk. The phone keeps ringing so much that finally my mom just lets it go to voice mail. The smells of pumpkin and chocolate waft from the ovens.

"This is the best day," Mom says, putting her arm around me. I lean into her and watch as Gram zips Tally into a long blue dress. The kitchen is so warm and bright that we barely notice the rain still pounding on the roof.

Gram drops us off at Tally's house on her way home. "Your mom is the coolest," Tally says, twirling in her dress in front of the long mirror on the back of her bedroom door. She and my mother agreed upon a dark green velvet one with a long skirt.

I shrug and pull open her closet door to hang up the other dresses. I stop, not sure what to do. The inside of her closet is worse than I had imagined. I look back at Tally, who has stopped twirling. It suddenly feels too close, too quiet. Then Tally comes and takes the dresses from me. She hangs them up on the empty rod and firmly pushes the door closed. "Anyway," Tally says, but then she doesn't say anything else. She just stares at her toenails, which she's painted a bright shade of acid green—one last sign of the old Tally. "I guess I'd better change out of this." She goes into the bathroom and shuts the door, leaving me still standing in the middle of her nearly empty room.

Inside the closet were three suitcases, lying open and perfectly packed. Full of all the stuff that's not in her room. For all of her talk about enjoying her time here and making the best of it, she's still waiting, ready to go at a moment's notice.

I raise my hand to knock on the bathroom door, but I can hear Tally sniffling. To give myself—and Tally—a little time to think about what to say, I go to the kitchen and get something to drink. Poppy is sitting at the kitchen table, wrapping one of her witch balls in bubble wrap. She looks up and smiles when I walk in. I sit in one of the other chairs and watch her work.

"That one came out really nice," I say as she picks up one

swirled in oranges and reds. She holds it up to the light. "It's a tree," I say, seeing the brown glass threaded from the bottom and opening up into a series of glass branches at the top.

"I was afraid it only looked like a tree to me." She twirls it, and we both watch as the tree slowly turns, the colors on its glass leaves catching the light as it spins.

"No, it's definitely a tree," I say. "Are there others?" Poppy nods and points to one of the boxes on the table. I peer inside, seeing another tree captured in colored glass. Instead of fall leaves, this one is covered with leaves in shades of green and yellow.

"Summer is there," she says, pointing to a ball swirled with pink and blue. I touch it, lightly feeling the unevenness of hand-blown glass. She wraps the autumn ball, folding bubble wrap over and around it until I can barely see the colors within.

"What about winter?" I ask.

"I haven't done winter yet," Poppy says. "It's been giving me some trouble. Winter trees are hard. They're just nothing, nothing but brown sticks poking up out of the ground."

"You should walk through Central Park in the winter," I say. "The trees there are amazing."

Poppy tilts her head at me. "Tell me," she says.

I close my eyes to really picture them and start telling her. I think about the last time my parents and I walked through the park at dusk, making our way home from uptown, where we'd spent the day. I tell her about the white snow frosting the branches and the blue light of the icicles dripping below. I describe how the evergreens reflect in the ice. I tell her about the purples that night brings to the trees.

"Wow," Poppy says, making me open my eyes. Tally is standing in the doorway, a faraway look on her face, like she's trapped in her own memory. And I know my face must look the same way, half haunted by something. I wonder what she's thinking about. Underneath it all, does she feel sad, like I do? That sadness you feel when you realize that the last time you did something was really the last time. And how you wish someone could have told you it was the last time, so you could pay extra attention. So you could really memorize it, because the memories were going to have to last forever.

"I'll walk you home," Tally says. Now she looks like the Tally I'm used to. It's weird how she can just flip like that. Poppy smiles at me and tucks the autumn ball into a box, taping it shut. "Did you bring in the mail yet?" Tally asks. Poppy shakes her head. "I'll check it on the way out," Tally says. I follow her down the hall, but not before I see the look on Poppy's face. Almost broken. She seems to have her own secret, her own sadness.

Tally jogs to the end of the driveway while I take my time, breathing in the fog that is rolling off the water. Tally opens the mailbox and dips her hand inside. She flips through the envelopes, then shoves them back into the box. "Nothing," she says when I reach her. Her voice is brittle, as if defying me to disagree. We go down to the beach and walk slowly along the sand, our heads down against the wind.

"My dad used to send me letters." Tally stops and kicks at a mussel shell. "Sometimes he'd put things in them, like a guitar pick or one of his set lists."

I think about the collage we made for Miss Beans's class. Knowing these were all gifts from her dad makes me think her project really was about Tally after all.

"One time he sent me a dollar bill folded like a bow tie." She smiles over at me.

"When was the last time you heard from him?" I ask gently.

She stares out at the water. "Three months ago."

"Oh," I say, feeling guilty. I start feeling anxious when I haven't heard from my dad in three *days*. "Have you written him?" I ask. She nods and tucks her chin into the neck of her coat. "He's always traveling. Maybe he just hasn't gotten them," I say.

"Maybe." We stand there for a long time just watching the waves. "Does your dad write you?" Tally asks.

"Some," I say. "No letters, though. Just e-mails." When we moved here I made a folder to save them. There are only five e-mails in it. Five in five months. And the last one came just last night. "Why don't you e-mail your dad?" I ask. "Or call him?"

"He doesn't do e-mail," she says, shrugging. "I've tried to call, but—" I nod. "Listen, I should get back," Tally says. She turns once and waves as she walks away, but then she disappears into the fog.

"See you," I call after her. I wish I could do more for her. I know a little about how she's feeling. The calls are the worst. You know they've gotten the message, so when they don't call back, it feels horrible in steps. Day One, you feel hopeful. Day Two, you tell yourself he's busy. Day Three, you realize he's just ducking you. I don't know what you tell yourself on Month Three.

The first thing I do when I get home is read Dad's e-mail again.

> Hi, Bean
> Great news. Mom and I talked, and everything's cool.
> Now we just have to work out some details, like timing.
> Can't wait to see you!
> Loads of love,
> Dad

"Penny!" Gram calls from the kitchen. "Phone."

I pick up the phone, expecting it to be my father. I've been trying to reach him by phone ever since I got the e-mail. But it's not him. It's Miss Beans.

"I just couldn't wait until tomorrow to tell you, Penny," she says quickly. "Your design for the float won."

I don't quite know what to say, so I say that. "I don't know what to say." I never expected to win. I thought my design was way too *random,* as Tally said. It is cool, though, that someone thinks it's good enough.

"It's going to be a lot of work," Miss Beans says. "But you'll have help. The whole art class will all help." She pauses. "Well, most of them." I can just imagine the reaction from the back table when Miss Beans announces that my float won. "I know it's been hard for you—being new. Which makes it all the more amazing how you've captured this year's theme." She goes on to list details about the trailer location and the farmer who said we could use his barn as a workshop.

I think about all of the things I included in my design. The things that I like about Hog's Hollow. All the things that do actually make this *the way life should be.* It's a little ironic that it may end up carrying one of the big things I don't like about Hog's Hollow: Charity. Of course just thinking about Charity's reaction makes me even happier about winning. Although I'm sure she'll make me pay somehow . . .

"I think a lot of people are going to respond to it. I know I did," Miss Beans continues.

"You did?"

"Definitely. It reminded me of why I wanted to move here in the first place."

"Really?"

"Life here can be—challenging. It's nice to be reminded of all the amazing things we've got."

I want to hear more about how it's hard for her, but then our call waiting beeps. "Miss Beans, I'm sorry, but I have to go."

"Of course, Penny," she says. "We'll talk more tomorrow in class."

This time it *is* my dad. I carry the phone out onto the back porch and sit in one of the chairs overlooking the water.

"Glad I caught you, Bean," he says. He sounds breathless, and I can hear city noises in the background—cars passing, horns blaring. It's weird to hear those sounds out here, where it's so quiet. "Did you get my e-mail?" he asks.

I nod but then realize he can't hear my head moving. "Yeah," I say.

"So, have you had a chance to think about things?"

I squint out at the beach, thinking I see a dog running by. It's hard to tell, because it's starting to get dark. "What things, Dad?" I ask, standing up. It's not a dog, just a wisp of fog rolling across the sand.

"About moving back," he says. A car horn blares and I hear someone shouting.

"Dad," I say, looking down at the porch, "what are you talking about?"

"Hasn't your mother talked to you?" he asks.

"About what?" I ask.

There's another loud screech and he curses under his breath. I don't know whether he's swearing at my mother or at something happening around him. "She said she'd talk to you." I hear more car horns and then people talking close by him.

"Talk to me about what?" I ask, feeling like we're just going in circles.

"About moving back to the City," my dad says. "You do still want to, right?"

I start thinking about seven things at once. About Tally and her suitcases, the parade float, the bakery, Marcus. "I guess . . . ," I say finally, because it has been what I've wanted for so long. There are now so many background noises on the phone that it is hard to figure out what the sounds are exactly.

"I just thought you'd be excited," he says. And his voice is softer now, making me sorry I didn't give him the answer he wanted.

"I am," I say. "I'm just . . ." I pause again. I'm just what? Unsure? Scared? Confused? "Surprised," I say. *Does this mean they're getting back together? Not selling the apartment?*

"Yeah," my father says quietly. Then it sinks in that all this time, he's been alone. Mom and I have barely been speaking to each other, but at least we've been together.

"Can I call you back later?" I ask. "I just need to . . ." Think. Talk to Mom. Stand and stare at the water.

"Of course," he says. "We'll talk later. I'm about to go down into the subway anyway." There is another horn, this time louder, right in my ear. "Can I call you tomorrow?" he asks.

"Yes," I say.

"Okay, then." He pauses again, letting the sounds of the city push through. "I love you, Bean," he says.

"I love you, too, Dad," I say. But the line is dead before I can say good-bye, so I'm not sure if he heard me.

chapter twenty-two

*T*ally comes by the house early to walk with me to school. She munches on the blueberry muffin Gram gave her as we left the house. I just hold mine as we walk. "Your mom must go into work really early," she says. "Poppy isn't even out of bed when I leave in the morning." She takes another bite of muffin.

"She's not at the bakery," I say. Tally looks over at me, but I don't say anything.

"Okay, I give up. Where is she?" Her voice is playful, like she's wants to make a game out of it.

"She's at another meeting in the City," I say.

Tally stops on the bridge and stands in front of me. "So, what's the deal?" she asks.

I shrug. This is not a conversation I want to have before school.

"Penny," Tally says. "What's going on?"

I shake my head. My eyes feel hot. I try to push past her, but she blocks my way.

"Just talk to me," she says, lowering her voice.

"Stop it," I say. I step around her and walk toward the sidewalk. Unfortunately, Tally follows me.

"Penny, whatever it is—"

I turn quickly. "Since you're such good friends with my mom now, why don't you ask her?" My voice is angry, but Tally doesn't back down. "She'll tell you they're separated, which everyone knows is just the first step toward getting a divorce."

"Maybe all the meetings in the City are them trying to work things out."

"Yeah, and if they do, you know what that means? It means we're moving back to the City. That's what my dad wants."

Tally's tone starts to match mine. "And it's what you want, too, right?"

"It's not that simple. You're the one with the suitcases packed and waiting, not me."

Tally's face is suddenly hard. "I was just trying to help," she says. She tosses the rest of her muffin to the ducks floating under the bridge.

"No," I say. "You were just trying to spin things. At some point, you just have to accept reality. Even if it sucks." I toss my muffin to the ducks, too, and walk off the bridge. This time Tally doesn't follow me.

When Miss Beans announces that my float won the contest, it has the effect I expected. Charity glares at me, but I just look away. I have bigger things to worry about. Miss Beans passes a sign-up sheet around the room. People are supposed to choose which element they will build for the float. I notice that no one at the back table even looks at the paper before passing it along. No surprise there.

Tally writes her name on one of the blanks then hands me the sheet without looking at me. It's almost full, which surprises me. The support, especially from Tally after I was so horrible, just makes me sadder, and it's all I can do to keep from crying.

Miss Beans suggests that we all meet at the Bealses' barn this weekend, looking at me for confirmation. I nod but wonder whether I'll be packing up my stuff this weekend. I don't even know which apartment we'd be moving back to—his new one, our old one, or a different one? The thing is, I have trouble even imagining my parents together again. It's been so long since they were happy. It's definitely time for all of us to talk. I tried to call each of my parents when I got to school, but both of their lines clicked immediately over to voice mail.

Tally doesn't wait for me when the bell rings. She just walks out without glancing back. Blake pauses at the door, but I look away. When I glance back up, he's gone. I decide to spend lunchtime in the library instead of the cafeteria. At least then I can be alone. I sit at the back table and open a book in front of me.

All that talk about Thanksgiving and too many orders was just a game. *Mom and I talked,* Dad said in his e-mail. If my mom knew we were moving back to the City, why couldn't she have told me, then? *Now we just have to work out the details.* It's yet another thing that my parents are going to make happen *to* me. No discussion. No asking what I want.

I hear talking on the other side of the bookcase. Just voices, no words. But it's the voices that make me stand up and look. Marcus and Charity are sitting together, their heads bent over a book. I watch for a moment, feeling the pit in my stomach get even bigger. I shut the book I was pretending to read and pick up my backpack. I get up too fast, knocking the chair over. I don't bother to pick it up when I run out of the library. I don't stop when I hear Marcus calling my name either.

I walk as fast as I can to the restroom, keeping my face down. Most people are still outside, eating lunch, so the halls are mostly empty. I lock myself in the last stall and lean against the door. Everything that could go wrong has. Just when I start to take some comfort in that fact, I find I'm wrong yet again.

The door to the restroom opens and closes. Hard-soled shoes click on the floor, heading my way. "I know you're in here." I hold my breath. She can't mean me. The footsteps stop on the other side of the stall door. "You might as well come out," she says. "I'm not leaving."

I sigh and close my eyes. "Why? So you can rub it in?"

She's quiet and for a brief moment I hope that she has silently floated away, but again I'm wrong.

"Just come out," she says.

I sigh and turn the latch. Charity is leaning against the sink with her arms folded.

"What do you want?" I ask. I am surprised that my voice isn't defeated, like I feel, but angry.

"I want you to get out of my life," she says, without missing a beat.

"Why do you hate me so much?" I ask.

"Because you were born," she says. "Ever since you came to town, you've been in my way, starting with my birthday and all the way up to today, when you were spying on me in the library."

"Excuse me for reading."

"Reading? What, no lunch? No lard à la mode?" she asks, smirking.

"You were the one who fell for that, not me."

"Well, you and your friend's lame tricks aren't going to stop me from winning." She jabs her finger at me. "You can tell her she has zero chance. People like you and her don't even belong here."

"We wouldn't dream of taking anything away from you,

Charity," I say flatly. There's no point in explaining to her that Tally is doing it for charity.

"Right. Like you didn't take my boyfriend?" She narrows her eyes at me.

This takes me by surprise. "What? Marcus is always hanging out with you," I say.

She glares at me. "You're so stupid, Penny."

"What are you talking about?"

She stares at me with her arms folded, then pushes away from the sink. "No, you know what? You are just going to have to find out how stupid you are on your own, because I have better things to do than hang around and talk to a loser like you." She walks out the door before I can say anything else.

I decide to take the rest of the day off. By *decide* I mean instead of going to fifth period, I just walk out and keep walking. I turn onto the now familiar dirt road off Main Street. I stop and look at the finished Jupiter, finding the seam that Mr. Fish was working on when I gave him and Marcus the cupcakes. Without the scaffolding, it seems smaller, more fragile. I keep hiking the uneven trail, following the distinctive tracks of Marcus's four-wheeler. I'm tired of having my life spun for me. First by my parents, and then by Charity and her friends. Even Marcus. I'm not even sure why I came up here, but it feels like I'm away from everything. I can see why Mr. Fish traded the beach for the woods.

It's so quiet that the sudden clank of a hammer startles me. I have to scramble up the last bit of hill, grabbing onto rocks with my hands. I pull myself up over the lip of the rise and see the curve of the skeleton that will eventually become the sixth planet.

Mr. Fish is bent over a sheet of paper that he has spread out over a big rock. I clear my throat so I won't startle him. He looks around quickly but smiles as soon as he sees me. "What are you doing up here?" He pulls his sleeve back and checks his watch. "Playing hooky?"

I nod and walk over to him. He searches my face for a long moment, and for a second it seems like he's going to ask me something, but then he turns to the paper spread in front of him again. "Well, I am not condoning skipping school, but it's good that you came along. I could use some help." I look at the paper where he's pointing and see that it's a huge schematic drawing of Saturn, complete with enormous rings. It's covered with arrows and notes, little reminders and warnings. *Watch this joint. Don't forget to add support here.* His finger rests on one of the junctions between the planet and the rings. "I can't seem to make this look like it's floating *around* the planet instead of hanging from it." I tilt my head and look at the drawing, remembering that I had the same dilemma with my cupcake.

"Well, you saw what I did," I say. I had to use little threads of sugar to attach the rings. "Maybe it's okay if you can see the supports. I mean, it's not like people are going to think that it's magically just hanging there." He smiles at me a little. "Maybe instead of making it like it should be, just make it like it is." He nods and looks back at his drawing.

"Marcus told me you were smart," he says. I blush when he says it. "I'm glad he has a friend like you."

Had *a friend like me,* I think. I look at the toes of my boots. "Can I ask you a question, Mr. Fish?"

"You just did," he says with a quick grin. "Go ahead. I'll answer you the best I can. Although I'd be the first to admit that I don't have all the answers."

"What made you do all of this?" I ask, pointing to the metal skeleton of Saturn.

"Note to self," he says, pretending to write on the paper in front of him. "Beware of Penny's questions." He sighs and leans against the rock, looking out into the hills.

"You don't have to . . . ," I begin, but he raises his hand.

"I'm just trying to tell *myself* why I did it in one thousand words or less." He smiles over at me. "The easy answer is: I had to." He pauses, looking at his hands. "When my wife died, Marcus and I went into a free fall. We needed something to hold on to. Something that connected us to her."

Like a lifeline, I think. *I could use one of those right about now.* "It's amazing," I say, looking out over the hills, where Venus is just catching the afternoon light.

"It is." He pauses and then laughs. "That makes me sound like an egomaniac. I meant the idea is amazing," he says. "The execution?" He looks behind him at Saturn. "Fair."

"I think it's good," I say. "Really good."

He shrugs. "Thank you," he says. "It has been good for me. But I'm ready to be finished." He smiles and looks over at me. "So what's with the questions?"

"I'm just trying to figure some things out," I say.

"Life things?" he asks. I nod. "Life can be pretty hard." I nod again, afraid I'm going to start crying if I speak. He's right. Even though my life is nowhere near as hard as his or Marcus's—or Tally's, for that matter—it *is* hard. "I'd like to tell you it gets easier," he continues, "but it doesn't. It just gets different."

"It's hard when things don't happen like you think they're supposed to," I say.

He looks up at Saturn for a long moment. "I guess at some point you just have to let go of what you thought should happen and live in what *is* happening." He runs his hand through his hair, just like Marcus. Then he turns to me. "I know it's not easy, though."

"That's for sure," I agree. We both stand there, examining the sixth planet. I try to imagine it all finished, but can't. For now, it's just a big jumble of metal pipes.

"Now, I would be neglecting my duties as a grown-up and parent if I didn't give you a ride back into town." He points toward his truck, which is parked down the hill on a dirt road I didn't even know existed. He rolls up his sketch and pushes it back into a long cardboard tube, which he tucks under his arm. "Ready?" he asks. I nod and follow him down the hill, hopping over several frozen puddles as I go.

"Are you excited about the festival?" he asks once we're inside the truck.

I think about my float, about all the things hanging off it. Things that have come to mean so much to me in such a short time.

"I am," I say, and I realize it's the truth. I just hope I'm still here to go to it.

Mr. Fish drives slowly, steering carefully through the deep ruts. Even so, we bounce around so much that I have to hang on to the handle above the door. When we reach the paved road, he turns to me.

"Where to?" he asks. "Home or school?"

"Actually, could you drop me at the bakery?" I ask. "I need to talk to my mom."

"Sure thing," he says.

When we pull up to the door, I thank him for the ride. "Sorry to take you away from your work," I say.

He waves the thought away. "It's good for a guy to come back down to earth every once in a while. And this is a tasty destination." He points to the bakery window. "I like that your mom named the place after you."

I look at him, surprised.

"Don't tell me you don't know," he says. "*You* are The Cupcake Queen. It's a well-deserved title, I must say." He waves as he pulls away.

The CLOSED sign is on the front door when he drops me off, so I have to go around to the back. It's cold in the kitchen. My mother is sitting with her back to me, her head in her hands.

I take a deep breath. "I want to know what's going on," I say before I have a chance to lose my nerve. My mother turns to look at me. Her eyes are puffy and red. She sniffs slightly and tries to smile but can't quite make it happen. "Hi," I say. It comes out soft. Almost a whisper.

"Hi," she says just as quietly.

"You're back early."

She looks at me and then at the clock over the sink. "You're out of school early."

I sit down on the stool across from the table without saying anything.

She looks back down at the table. "I should have talked to you long ago." She sniffs again and reaches into her pocket, pulling out a very crumpled tissue. "I was just waiting for the right time."

I almost ask why in five months there wasn't a good time. But I keep my mouth shut. I want to hear what she's been waiting so long to say. She takes a deep breath. "All these meet-

ings your father and I've been having . . . they're about you."
She looks back up at me. She seems to be searching my face for
something.

"We're moving back," I say.

She seems surprised. So surprised that I know I'm wrong.

"No," she says. "*We* aren't." She sniffs again into her tissue.

"What do you mean?" I ask. "Dad said—"

"Penny." She sighs. "Your father and I are getting a divorce."

And there it is. The announcement that I've been waiting
for, bracing myself for. I wait for the tears to come, but they
don't. I just feel numb.

"The meetings . . . your father wants you to come live with
him," she says, gazing just past me, like I'm already gone. "He
said you and he talked about it." She looks right at me, her eyes
wet now. "He said you begged him to let you come back."

I feel off balance and grab onto the table for support. I think
of the e-mails, the voice-mail messages. The conversation we
had weeks ago. All that time I wanted *us* to go back. Not just
me. I wanted all of us to be in the same place. I kept thinking
if I could push their lives closer to each other, they'd figure out
how to put our old life back together. But maybe this was as
much as they could do. Half.

"We have a good life here, don't we?" Mom says.

I nod. She's right. Aside from a few things, it *is* a good life.

"Is it that you miss your dad?"

"I do miss him, but . . ." I shrug.

"What is it, then, Penny?"

"It's just not the life I thought I'd have," I say. I think about what Mr. Fish said about how sometimes life isn't what you thought it would be. It's just what it is.

"I know. It isn't for any of us," my mother says. I see teardrops on the table in front of her. I want to say something that will make it stop hurting for her, but the gap between us has gotten so big that I don't know how to reach her.

"So, what now?" I ask.

She sits up straighter, like she's bracing herself. "It's your decision," my mother says. "At fourteen, it's your choice."

"But, I'm not—"

"You will be by the time all of this is done," she says.

"So, I'm just supposed to choose?" I ask. "Choose between my own parents?" If someone had asked me two months ago whether I wanted to stay here or move back to the City, it would have been a much easier choice. Then my mother would have been the only thing holding me here. Now? There are a lot of things. I just hope I haven't wrecked some of those things forever.

"I've gotta go somewhere right now, Mom, okay?"

She stretches out her arm. "Don't go, Penny. We just started talking. I know how hard this is on you," she says.

I shake my head. "You have no idea."

My mother looks down. "You're right. I can only imagine."

I stand up and tuck my stool under the table. "I need to go," I say.

From the expression on her face, it looks like she thinks I'm talking about forever.

"We'll talk later, okay? I promise," I say.

"Okay," she says.

And this time we both mean it.

chapter twenty-three

Tally answers the door when I knock. "What do you want?" she asks.

"Can you come out?"

She looks at me for a moment, then—thankfully—she nods. "Give me a second," she says, stepping back into the house. She returns quickly, zipping up her purple fleece. We walk slowly up the driveway toward the road. Tally doesn't even pause as we pass the mailbox.

"I'm sorry," I say. "I shouldn't have talked to you the way I did. I was a jerk."

"You're right," she says, and I wince a little. We walk past the Cathances' driveway, leaning into the wind. "But I shouldn't have pushed you. I should have just let you tell me when the time was right."

"There's never a good time to tell someone their parents are getting a divorce." Now I sound like my mother.

Tally looks over at me. "Divorced? Really?"

"Yeah, my mom just told me," I say. We walk past the Fishes' driveway, then past Gram's. As it starts to drizzle, I tell her my dad wants me to move in with him. "They say it's my choice."

"You've been wanting out of Hog's Hollow ever since you got here," Tally says. Her voice is flat when she says it. I look at her, but she keeps her chin tucked into the neck of her fleece, watching the ground in front of her. "I guess you got what you wished for."

"I didn't wish for this," I say. We step off the road and make our way down toward the water. We stop, looking out past the point, where the lighthouse is making its slow turns, sending its beams into the fog. "Nothing is the way it's supposed to be," I say. "I mean, how am I supposed to choose between my own parents?"

Tally stares out into the fog. "You just pick, I guess," she says. Her voice is tight, like it hurts her to talk.

I look over at her, but she won't meet my gaze. "Tally, are you still mad at me?" I ask. "I said I was sorry." Then it hits me. "If I move, I'll still visit," I say.

Tally laughs, but like her words, it's hard and sharp. "Penny, both of your parents want you to live with them. Having two people fighting over you is a *good* problem to have," she says. "What if neither of them wanted you?" On her face, tears are mixing with the rain.

"Tally, your dad is coming back. He's just busy," I say. "He'll contact you soon."

She shakes her head. "Now who's spinning things?" She pushes her hand into the pocket of her fleece and pulls out an envelope that's been folded in half. "The problem with spinning things is that you can get too good at it. You can make it seem real, so real that even you start to believe it. But underneath, the truth is still there."

She unfolds the envelope and hands it to me. I recognize Tally's handwriting on the front, her careful letters, the slight upward slant. It's addressed to someone with the same last name who lives in Seattle. Right over the address and her father's name is a big red stamp. DELIVERY REFUSED. RETURN TO SENDER.

"Tally . . . ," I begin. I pause, not sure what to say. What kind of father does that to his daughter? "I'm so sorry."

Tally looks at me for a long moment, then out at the lighthouse on the point, its beams trying to cut through the fog. "It hurts," she says. "A lot."

I just nod. Like my mother said to me, *I can only imagine.*

"But, in a way it's good," she says. She laughs when she sees the shock on my face. "I'm not spinning. I swear," she says, raising her right hand. "It's just good to know where you stand, you know?"

I think about my mom's announcement and how long I've been waiting for it, dreading it. "I guess it is better to know for sure what you're up against," I say.

"Yeah, better than hoping every day, just to get a nasty surprise." She takes the envelope back from me, rips it up into little pieces, and throws them into the ocean.

Watching the pieces float away seems to make her feel better. "Speaking of nasty surprises, find anything new in your locker today?" she asks.

"I didn't stay long enough to find out." Then I tell her about Charity's talk with me in the girls' room.

"Oh, well, at least the lard worked for a little while . . . ," Tally says with an evil smile. Then she sees the worry on my face. "You know, there's only one way for you to find out what's going on with Marcus."

"I know." But there's something else I need to do first. Something more important.

My mom is sitting at the kitchen table, talking on the phone, when I get back to Gram's. "I have to go," she says, and clicks it off. "Are you okay?" she asks.

"Yeah," I say, realizing I am. I unzip my coat and slide it off.

"Are you staying awhile?" my mother asks. That's an old joke between us, *Take off your jacket and stay awhile.*

"I am, Mom," I say. "I'm staying."

She looks at me for a long moment. For the first time in a long time, she looks exactly as she should. Exactly like the mom I remember. And when she hugs me, it feels exactly right, too.

chapter twenty-four

The wind is cold on the walk over to Tally's house and it smells like it's going to snow. The idea of going into the bakery extra early this morning was my mom's. The design was mine. I have to shift the box I'm carrying to one hand when I knock. Poppy opens the door.

"Come in, come in," she says. She has her hair pulled away from her face under a handkerchief, just like the first time I met her. "Tally's not here, but I want you to see something." I follow her into the kitchen, putting my box on the island. She walks to the window hung with her witch balls and touches one speckled with purples and blues and silvers. A long dark trunk grows out of the bottom of the ball, touching the colors dancing across the top. "What do you think?" she asks.

"It's perfect," I say, and it is. It looks exactly the way I remember. I keep looking at the ball, thinking about my decision not to go back. It makes me sad to think that part of my life is gone, that things will never be the same, but like Tally, at least now I know what I'm dealing with.

"Tally's over at the ARK," Poppy says. I had forgotten she's there every Saturday. "I'll drive you over. I know she wants to see you." Poppy smiles. "And I know she would want whatever is in that box." I reach over and lift up the top so Poppy can take a peek. "They're perfect," she says. "You really are the Cupcake Queen."

I laugh. "That's what Mr. Fish said, too."

"Really?" She looks surprised, then pleased. "How's he doing these days?"

"Good," I say. "Though I think he's going to have a lot of free time on his hands soon."

"Sounds like he needs to find a new project," Poppy says.

"Maybe he could help you design some planet witch balls," I suggest.

"Hmm," Poppy says thoughtfully as she walks over and picks up her keys.

"Unless you prefer working alone . . ."

"Two heads are often better than one," she says. "Look how you helped me with winter."

"Oh, that reminds me, could I make a call before we go?" I ask.

Gram sits in the front seat with Poppy while I sit in the back, the box of cupcakes balanced on my lap. I knew Tally would be disappointed if I didn't at least try to get Gram to come with us. The ARK is exactly like I thought it would be and nothing like I thought it would be. I was picturing something like the shelter where we adopted Oscar, a big gray building that looked blah enough to be a warehouse. The ARK is actually in someone's house, or part of it. I leave the cupcakes in the car and follow Gram and Poppy around to the back of the house. When Gram and I walk in, there are about twenty cats, sunning themselves on the windowsills, chasing little Wiffle balls across the floor, or climbing up the sides of carpeted condos. The whole room is filled with cats, living in what has to be cat heaven. Tally walks out from the house part of the ARK with a plastic pitcher full of cat food and a stack of plastic bowls.

"You came!" Tally says. She has ditched her "normal" look. When she walks toward me, the sun catches her hair, which is streaked in not one, but all three primary colors. She's wearing green tights with denim shorts and a jacket that once belonged to someone named VINNIE. I raise my eyebrows at her, which makes her laugh. She puts me right to work, handing me the bowls and pointing out where they go. She follows me around, tipping a bit of food into each. Gram picks up a Wiffle ball and tosses it for a tiny white kitten, who chases it down and actually returns it to Gram.

"Smart cat," I say, placing the final bowl on one of the windowsills.

Tally opens the door to the rest of the house and calls, "Monica, I'll be right back."

A woman with long blond hair pulled back into a ponytail comes to the door, holding another stack of bowls. "You must be Penny," she says, pulling the door shut behind her. I nod, smiling. "I've heard good things," she says.

"I'm going to show her around," Tally says.

"I'll stay here," Gram says, tossing the ball again. She laughs as the kitten brings it back and drops it at her feet. Poppy picks up a big black cat and cuddles him in her arms. I wonder if he is destined to be cat number ten.

Tally and I head out to the backyard, where the rest of the animals are kept in several outbuildings. It's easy to tell which building houses the dogs.

"I'm staying," I say.

It's barely out of my mouth before Tally grabs my hands and starts jumping up and down. The strands of her hair float up and down as she jumps, making a rainbow around her head.

"So, what happened to your pageant look?" I ask when she finally stops jumping.

Tally shrugs. "I guess I just had what my dad used to call a Come-to-Jesus meeting."

"A what?"

"You know, just an honest heart-to-heart."

"With yourself?" I ask.

"Yup." She wrinkles her nose when she says it, making me laugh.

"Tally, you are an inspiration," I say, making her laugh.

"I should have my own television show," she says. *"Heart-to-Heart with Tally."*

I shake my head and smile. "So what now?" I ask.

"I'm just going to let my life be what it is, you know?"

I do know. "So, you're not doing the pageant? But what about the money for the ARK?"

"I'm totally doing it. I'm just doing it my way." She flips her hair with her hand, making the rainbow effect again. "Do you doubt my ability to win?"

I shake my head. I don't doubt much of anything anymore.

"You're still going to help me, right?"

"Absolutely," I say.

"Good, because I'm going to need a new dress and new shoes and . . ."

"They're not going to know what hit them," I say.

"You got that right." We walk through the dog building. The barking is so loud I have to cover my ears as we step inside. Tally pauses and greets each dog as we pass, offering a scratch behind the ears or a pat on the head. We walk all the way to the end and then out into the yard.

"What are in the other buildings?" I ask as we step back outside.

"That's just a storage shed," Tally says, pointing to the nearest building. "That one has rabbits, ferrets, and rodents." I squinch my nose up. We had a rat problem in our building in the City. I don't think I'll ever be able to think about rodents as pets.

"What about that one?" I ask.

"That one holds the exotics," Tally says, pointing to last building on the lot. We are about halfway there when something white and round comes barreling through the yard straight toward me. I barely have time to scream before it's on me. It hits my legs and bounces off. I look over at Tally, expecting her face to be a combination of terror and surprise, like mine, but she's just laughing. I look at the round ball of what I now can see are feathers. A completely bald pink head pokes out of the top of the ball. Matching pink feet poke out of the bottom.

"What is *that*?" I ask.

Tally is laughing so hard she can barely speak. I glare at her as the white thing hops around us in circles. "That's Snowball."

"What *is* Snowball?" I ask.

"She's a turkey vulture." Tally bends and taps Snowball on the beak, causing her to make a noise that sounds like a cross between a sick bullfrog and a creaking door. "She's sort of the ARK mascot." Tally straightens up, and Snowball hops over to me. "Pet her. She won't bite." I bend and tap Snowball on the head as Tally did. Snowball starts hopping across the yard to where Gram and Monica, followed by Poppy, are coming out of the back of the house. Tally bends and picks up an apple that has fallen from one of the trees. "Snowball lost both wings in a hunting accident."

"Whoa," I say. I watch as Monica bends to tap Snowball. Gram and Poppy each take a turn greeting her.

Tally nods. "But she's really happy here."

"Seems like you are, too," I say.

"Yeah," Tally says. "I am." She pauses and watches Snowball hop back toward the exotics building. "When I first moved here, I spent a lot of time just thinking about myself and my problems." I nod, feeling guilty. Even though she's talking about herself and not me, it's hitting close to home. "Here I get outside of myself, you know?" We start walking back toward the house.

"Yeah," I say, thinking I sometimes feel like that when I'm designing cupcakes. "I'll bet it's really expensive to keep this place running." I think of the twenty-dollar bill I have sitting in the top drawer of my desk.

Tally nods. "I need to win the pageant. That money could really make a big difference around here."

As we walk toward where Gram and Poppy are standing, I can see Gram holding the tiny white kitten in her hands. Tally reaches out to pet the purring kitten. "Someone seems really happy," she says.

"I know I am," says Gram.

"You're taking it?" I ask, joining in the petting. "What about Oscar? He might not be so happy about it."

"Oh, he will," Gram says. "Who could resist this face?" As if on cue, the little kitten gives a tiny meow. "Isn't she cute?" Gram asks. I smile and shake my head. Tally was right. She couldn't resist.

"What are you going to name her?" Tally asks.

Gram tilts her head to one side, studying the wriggling kitten. "Cupcake," she says with a big grin.

"That reminds me," I say, and I tell Tally to follow us to the car. I lift the box out of the backseat and hand it to her. She starts laughing as soon as she peeks inside. "Choose wisely," I say. This time I made an even dozen. Four of each design.

Tally lifts a cupcake with a big mound of chocolate on it out of the box. "Rock is my new favorite," she says before taking a big bite.

We climb back into Poppy's car, leaving Tally to finish up her rounds. I wave as we start to pull away.

"Wait!" Tally says, making Poppy stop. She hurries over to my window. "I almost forgot. Blake told me to tell you that Marcus is failing French."

I just look at her for a while, not sure how Marcus's academic status is relevant to anything. But then I realize what that means.

"Ohhh," I say. Tally backs away from the car, smiling.

"She's really great," I say, holding Cupcake in my lap as Poppy backs out of the driveway.

"Who?" Gram asks. "Cupcake, or Tally?"

I smile. "Both."

"I think you're right," Gram says. Cupcake meows in agreement, making us all laugh.

We turn onto the road, passing a clump of trees that have

turned orange. I smile when I think about Snowball, probably the weirdest animal I've ever seen. She lost both her wings and yet seems completely happy. I think about what Marcus and Mr. Fish lost, and Tally . . . and me, and how we all have to adapt, too.

The car kicks up the colored leaves as we make our way down the narrow road toward home. And it occurs to me that it's the first time I've thought of it like that. Home.

chapter twenty-five

*W*hen we got home, there was a message on my voice mail from Dad. Just a *Call me. We need to talk* message. I call him back after we get Cupcake settled in the laundry room. Monica said it would be best to ease into introducing her to Oscar. As it is, Oscar is just walking back and forth in front of the closed door, making weird noises in his throat.

"Hi, sweetheart," my dad says when he answers. He sounds a little nervous, which makes me nervous.

"Hi, Dad," I say. Oscar works half of one of his legs under the door, trying to touch Cupcake. I push him away and sit down in front of the door, where I can keep an eye on him. "I got your message," I say. I wonder if he knows Mom talked to me. I really don't want *that* announcement twice.

"Yeah," he says. I can hear a faint scratching sound through the phone. When I close my eyes I can see him smoothing his beard, his nervous habit. "I just wanted to see how you were feeling today," he says.

Now I'm guessing that Mom did talk to him. *Did she already tell him my decision?* "I'm okay," I say.

"Listen, Penny, we have to—"

"Dad," I say. I decide just to tell him. It's not like it's going to get any easier. "I'm going to stay here."

He's so quiet that I'm afraid the call dropped, but then I hear him take a breath. "Are you—?" Then he stops himself. "That must have been a hard decision," he says. All emotion seems to have drained from his voice.

"Yeah," I say. "It was." I pause for a moment, willing the tears to go back into my eyes. "Dad, I really miss you, and I want to see you. I just want to stay in one place for a while. Please understand."

He clears his throat. "I do. I'm sorry I jumped the gun. I got too excited, I guess. . . ."

This is almost worse than if he were really angry. "Dad, I want to come for a visit soon, okay?" I say.

"I'd really like that," he says. His voice sounds a little better. "Your mom and I talked about Thanksgiving. You know, my new place is right on the parade route."

"Cool," I say. "Can we go the night before and watch them blow up the huge balloons?"

"That sounds great to me," he says, and I can tell that he means it.

"Or we could just hang out . . . ," I offer. Oscar is back. He starts working his leg under the door again.

"Whatever you want to do," he says. Through the phone I can hear someone talking to my father. "Penny," he says, "can you hang on just a minute?" I start to say yes, but he's already talking to the other person, his voice muffled, like he has his hand over the mouthpiece.

I pull Oscar away from the door again, but as soon as I do, Cupcake slides her paw under the door. "Penny?" my dad says. "Listen, I need to call you later, okay? We'll work something out." His voice is so sad, so apologetic.

"Of course," I say. Oscar pulls away from me and goes over to the door and sniffs Cupcake's paw. "Dad?"

"Yeah, Bean?"

"I love you." Oscar puts his paw under the door, and when I bend down, I can see Cupcake sniffing his paw, too.

"I love you, too," he says. "Can't wait to see you."

"Me neither," I say. After I hang up, I sit there for a while, watching Oscar and Cupcake try to touch each other through the closed door.

After dinner, I decide to go for a walk on the beach. It's snowing a little, just a dusting. I've never seen it snow on the beach before. The snowflakes sit on the sand for a moment before melting. They look like the ones kindergartners make and hang in the school windows during the holidays. I hear a dog barking down the beach and wonder if—and hope that—it's Sam. I haven't seen Marcus since the library. So much has happened since yesterday.

Each of the houses along the beach has an automatic lantern at the top of its steps down to the sand. It's now dark enough for them to come on. Even the Fishes' place has its lantern lit.

"Hey," a voice says from above me.

I look up, but it's hard to see. I have to blink to keep the snow out of my eyes. "Marcus?" I say. I hear a soft chuckle, followed by Sam's whine. "What are you doing out here?" I walk over to the base of the steps to his old house.

"I could ask you the same thing," he says. "Want to come up?" Sam chuffs, and I can hear him straining against his collar.

I step onto the porch, careful of the third step, and sit. I put my hand out for Sam to lick. I think about making Marcus squirm for a bit. I don't understand why he didn't tell me about Charity for so long.

"So, I'm failing French," I say. I have to force myself not to look at him. "Madame says I need to get a tutor." I can barely keep a smile from my face.

Marcus takes a deep breath. "I'm failing French, too," he says.

I can't help it anymore. I start giggling.

"What's so funny?" Marcus asks. "Wait, you already knew, didn't you?"

I nod, still laughing.

"How did you—?"

"Small town," I say.

Marcus runs his hand through his hair. "I should have known," he says.

"You should have told me." All those times I saw him with Charity. Being tutored.

"I know. I mean, I wanted to. I started to." He talks fast, his words rushing against one another.

I put my hand on his arm. "It's okay," I say. "But no more secrets."

He smiles over at me, his eyes crinkling. "What about your birthday present? Can that be a secret?"

I nod. "But my birthday is still almost two months away," I say.

"That's a long time to keep a secret," he says. Marcus reaches over and takes my hand. "A nonbirthday present, then," he says. I feel something being placed around my wrist. When he releases it, I can see the bracelet he always wears is now on me.

"Thank you," I say.

"I made it this summer."

I touch the braided leather with my fingers. Knowing he made it himself makes it that much better. "Thank you."

"You already said that," Marcus says, laughing.

"Well, that makes it doubly true," I say.

He keeps holding my hand as we watch the snow falling on

the sand. "My mother had this poster. It was of the birth of a star." He looks at me. Sam looks up at me, too. I reach out and stroke his ears, but I keep watching Marcus. "Do you know what happens when a star dies?" he asks. I shake my head. "Stars don't just burn out. It's always a huge event. Sometimes they explode and leave a black hole that sucks in anything that comes near it." He shifts slightly, leaving space between us, and the side of my body where he was leaning is suddenly cold. "I think that's what happened to my dad and me when my mom died. It was like all of the light got sucked out of our universe." He is quiet again, and I hear the sounds of Sam's breathing and the waves pulling at the stones on the beach.

"What else can happen?" I ask. "You said 'sometimes.'"

He moves his foot out from under Sam's body. "Sometimes when it dies, it leaves part of itself behind. Bits that turn into other things."

"Like what?" I ask.

"Sometimes other stars. But every once in a while"—he glances over at me—"a dying star becomes a pulsar. One of the brightest stars."

We both look up, but there are no stars to see tonight, only a few lanterns fading into the snow flurries.

"I bet your mom was one of those kind," I say. "She had to be, if she inspired you and your dad so much."

Marcus smiles over at me. "You make me believe that's true."

I hear a car pull onto the driveway above us and Sam is off

my lap, pushing past me on the steps. He runs around the house toward the road. I hear the low creak of a truck door and then the sound of boots on gravel.

Marcus smiles and stands up, pulling me up with him. He puts his arms around me. "So, the dance . . . ," he says. As he talks I can feel his breath on my cheek, then in my hair.

I nod, smiling.

"Good," he says, pulling back slightly. "Now go. I don't want you to get grounded or anything."

I step down off the porch and turn and smile at him again through the falling snow.

"I'll see you tomorrow," he says. "I can't wait to get to work on your float."

"Marcus, you down there?" A voice calls from inside the house. Marcus looks at me and smiles. *Crinkle.*

I can't stop smiling. I don't even feel cold anymore.

"I'm right here, Dad," he says. He waves at me before walking across the porch.

I head up the beach, watching the fat snowflakes slowly sink into the sand. I turn and see a light go on inside the Fishes' place, then Mr. Fish silhouetted in the doorway. "Night, Miss Cupcake Queen!" he calls.

I wave and keep walking down the beach through the softly falling snow. The light glowing on Gram's path pulls me forward, beckoning me home.

I can see my breath even inside the barn. It's been snowing on and off for the last week, but Gram tells me this weekend is supposed to be warm (well into the fifties) and sunny. Not that it matters. In the fifty-three years they've been having the Hog's Hollow Days Festival, they've only canceled the parade once, and that was because there was a tornado warning.

Blake leans over the side of the float, painting the giant pair of scissors with silver paint. "The tornado picked up a cow and put it down a mile away." He sees the look on Tally's face. "It was fine. Just dizzy."

"Is that how they make a milk shake?" Tally asks, earning her a silver nose. I laugh but duck when Blake comes at me with the paintbrush. I finish adding the oversize sprinkles to a Styrofoam cupcake and step back to take a look at my work.

It's weird seeing my design in three dimensions. At first, I was worried that we wouldn't be able to get it finished. Last Sunday only Miss Beans, my mom, Poppy, Gram, Marcus, Tally, and Blake came to help. Late in the day about half a dozen people from my art class showed up, but the group has been growing slowly over the last week. There's probably about twenty-five here today, although it's hard to keep track of them. Someone's always off getting more paint or coffee or doughnuts—or a new blowtorch, when Mr. Fish's stopped working.

The door opens and someone else walks in. It's hard to tell who she is with her scarf wrapped around her face, but I recognize her voice as soon as she starts talking. "What can I do?" Charlotte asks, unwinding her scarf and removing her gloves. She gives me a small smile, which grows when I smile back. I direct her toward where my mom is fighting with the giant tomatoes.

"What do you think?" Gram asks, skewering another foam cupcake on one of the metal rods sprouting off the back of the float. She's covered in the silver glitter she used to decorate its top.

"Amazing," I say as she climbs down and heads off to help someone else. Mr. Fish mounted curved metal rods all around the trailer. At first it just looked like a really dangerous porcupine. The tomatoes were the first to make it on. They were pretty easy, even though Blake kept telling us that we had them all wrong. *More orange, more round, more tomato-y.* I helped Mr. Fish and Marcus with all of the Styrofoam planets. Mr. Fish smiled at me as he used skewers to attach Saturn's rings.

"See?" Tally says, walking over and linking her arm through mine. "I knew you had interesting stuff on the inside." The barn door slides open behind us, letting in a flurry of snow and a blast of cold air. Even dressed in a turtleneck, two sweaters, and a fleece, I still shiver. "I hope I get to stand at the back," she says, pointing to where the giant rock, paper, and scissors are mounted.

"I think you will. I mean, doesn't the winner get to stand up front?"

"Good thing the trailer has good shocks," she says. "There's going to be a lot of weight up front."

"I still can't believe it went on for as long as it did," I say, thinking of Charity stuffed into her long dress, looking more like a swollen sausage than a pageant contestant.

"Honestly, I can't believe they fell for it at all," Tally says. "I mean, lard? How dumb can you be?"

"And yet, Charity still won," I say. "Where's the justice in that?"

"Come on, Penny. You knew she'd win," Tally says. "She knew it, too."

I nod. Charity didn't look surprised when they put the crown on her head. She didn't even look that happy. After the pageant she just stood there frozen, holding her father's pudgy hand while her mother talked with everyone who came up to congratulate her. For like three seconds I felt sorry for her, but then she looked at me and mouthed something I'm pretty sure no real queen would ever say.

"I had hoped you'd be up front doing your whole British-monarchy-wave thing."

"Instead I will be at the back, smiling bravely along with the rest of the runner-ups. Losers, please move to the back." I poke Tally with my elbow, although she probably can barely feel it through all of my layers.

"First Runner-up isn't exactly losing."

"Should the Hog Queen be unable to meet her duties . . ."

"What *are* the Hog Queen duties?" I ask.

"Wave and smile? Oh, and eat a lot of sausage."

"I'm sorry you didn't win," I say. "I think you should have."

"I'm pretty sure you have to say that," Tally says. "It's part of the best-friend code." She shrugs. "The only thing I'm really bummed about is that the ARK won't get the money. But we'll figure something else out."

The door opens again. This time it's Marcus, carrying a big white bundle in his hands. He smiles at me from across the barn. Sam trots in behind him.

"So, are you going to walk with Oscar in the parade?" Tally asks. I smile at the image of my big, round cat at the end of a leash. I shake my head. Oscar would freak out from all the noise. Tally has about thirty people signed up to walk with their pets and collect money for the ARK along the parade route.

"Good," Tally says. "Because Monica dropped a bag of dog food on her foot and broke her toe."

"So she can't walk in the parade?" I ask, watching my mom laugh at something Blake said. Then what Tally's saying hits me. "Oh no," I say.

"Too late," Tally says. "I already told Monica you'd do it." I sigh. "Besides, Snowball would be really sad to miss the parade."

I roll my eyes. "Okay," I say. Walking a turkey vulture in the Hog Days' parade doesn't seem any weirder than anything else around here.

"You're still coming to my house after to get ready for the dance, right?"

"Yeah, but I did promise my mom we'd stop by on the way so she can take pictures. She promised she wouldn't embarrass me," I add.

"She *has* to embarrass you before your first dance. That's part of the mom code."

Tally seems mostly okay about not having one of her actual parents around. When you add my family and Blake's to Poppy, she has three kinda-mothers and a kinda-grandmother pestering her about eating enough and zipping up her coat when it's cold.

Tally and I stand together, watching the last few items get placed on the float. "I still think you should have put a can of lard on the float," she says. I elbow her and we both laugh. She walks over to where my mother is putting a crown on top of another cupcake. Mom smiles at me when she sees me looking at her.

Marcus hands Blake one end of the bundle he brought with him. They slowly unroll it, stretching it along the length of the float. I had to get permission to change the banner. At first they weren't going to let me, but then Miss Beans convinced them that it would improve "the aesthetic of the art" or something like that. Marcus nails one end in place and then walks to the other, making sure everyone can read it before he tacks it into place. My original plan for the float had included a banner, but it just stated the Hog Festival theme: HOG'S HOLLOW — THE WAY LIFE SHOULD BE. As I look around at all the people who have gathered to help put this together, I think the new banner is much better. I have to remember to e-mail a picture of the whole thing to my dad.

Poppy and Mr. Fish are standing near the back of the trailer, talking, their breath visible in the cold air. Blake and Tally are laughing near the doughnut box as he tries to beat his record for number of doughnut holes in his mouth at one time. Charlotte and Sam are playing tug-of-war with a drop cloth.

After Marcus finishes tacking the banner into place, he comes and stands near me, his hand finding mine. His writing is kind of crooked, but something about that seems right, too. Gram moves down the trailer, inspecting it closely to make sure that everything is secure enough to withstand the wind. Even though she's standing in front of the banner, I can still read it around her. HOG'S HOLLOW — THE WAY LIFE IS.

acknowledgments

Thank you to Stephanie Owens Lurie for being so smart, so kind, and always so generous. Thank you to Aimee Bissonette for talking me down off the many ledges. Thanks to everyone at Dutton Children's Books and Penguin Young Readers for their continuing support. (Especially to Julie Strauss-Gabel and Lisa Yoskowitz for adopting me and this book.) Thank you to Terry, my parents, and to Bob for having the grace to keep loving me even when I am so very unlovable. And finally thank you to Brad Barkley for telling me that I was ready and for always reminding me not to flail.